CALL ME DADDY

JADE WEST

Edited by John Hudspith   www.johnhudspith.co.uk
Cover design by Letitia Hasser of RBA Designs - http://designs.romanticbookaffairs.com/
All enquiries to jadewestauthor@gmail.com

First published 2017

Judge by the title.

If you think this book might not be for you, then you're probably right.

If you're already wet at the prospect, then I hope you enjoy the ride.

Love, Jade <3

This book is dedicated to guilty pleasures, pink glitter and daddy issues.

CHAPTER ONE

Laine

My stupid pumps aren't cut out for this weather. Cold water squelches between my toes, and my breath is misty, wet hair like frozen straw against my cheeks. I can hardly see through the rain.

Damn my birthday for being so late in November.

Damn me for not thinking harder about my wardrobe choices.

I wasn't planning on being out this late, eighteenth birthday or not. I'm dressed for a quick coffee on a cloudy afternoon, not for clubbing through a stormy evening – leggings and a strappy cami under a fluffy teal cardigan that holds more rain than it keeps out. This stupid scenario is all Kelly Anne's fault, insisting it wouldn't be a proper birthday celebration unless it involved getting trashed in some sleazy club in the backstreets of Brighton. *We'll have a great time,* she said, *just a bus ride and a couple of drinks,* she said. *Who knows, you may even meet someone hot and finally ditch the V card,* she said.

I have no intention of trading my virgin status for a drunken fumble in a back alley with some random who barely knows my name.

1

And now she's bailed on me, typical Kelly Anne style. Last I saw of her she was lip-locked with some vest-top-clad hipster with thick-rimmed glasses. Then she was gone, off in a puff of tequila-scented pheromones for some bump and grind at hipster-guy's pad, no doubt. Regular, except she still has my phone, purse and keys in her handbag for safekeeping.

My own stupid fault for believing for one single second she'd take care of them. Nothing is safe with Kelly Anne after a couple of tequilas, despite what she'll have you believe.

I root through my sopping pockets, nothing there but a couple of soggy cigarette papers.

Idiot, I'm such an idiot.

I have no real plan for getting home to Newhaven. It's the best part of a ten-mile hike, and the odds of making it back without either succumbing to hypothermia or stumbling into the sea are slim to nil. I'm sure I should be more freaked out than I am, but I feel strangely nonchalant. Actually, it's more numb than nonchalant. Maybe I've had a few too many tequilas myself, or maybe it's the sorry knowledge that I have nobody who cares enough to realise I'm stranded all alone without a penny in my pocket.

The fact that Kelly Anne is my best friend and the only real person who gave a shit about my birthday says it all. Even if I do make it home tonight, there'll be nobody there. Mum's away again, off in France with her latest conquest. Denny, he's called. He works over there, doing up properties for rich folk, giving Mum the illusion that she's one of them, and that's all she's ever wanted. That and a man who'll stick with her longer than it takes to shoot his load. So far so good with Denny, six months and going strong. At least she remembered my birthday enough to send a text this year.

I think I'm heading for the sea front, I *hope* I'm heading for the sea front. They have bars there that stay open all night, maybe I can find somewhere to hang out until morning, somewhere vaguely warm to pass the time until I figure something out – except I don't have my

ID, that's in Kelly Anne's handbag, too. Even if I had any money for a drink, nobody ever lets me buy one without ID. I still get half-fare on public transport, that's how young I look. Kelly Anne says it's because I'm so blonde. *You look like one of those creepy porcelain dolls*, she says, *but prettier*. I guess that's supposed to be a compliment.

Maybe I should try to find a police station, explain my sorry situation and hope they'll let me stay until morning. Maybe I could face the ten-mile hike home when the sun comes up, if it ever stops raining. Maybe I could find a way to break in at home, or I could head over to Kelly Anne's and wait for her to resurface, give her a piece of my mind for leaving me up shit creek on my own birthday without so much as loose change to my name. Maybe her parents will be home, maybe they'll let me dry off and wait it out in her bedroom.

My numb feet splash through a puddle and it turns out they aren't as numb as I thought. My teeth are chattering, arms folded tight, my wet cardigan so cold against my skin that it feels like an ice bath. Everything seems darker here. I can't hear any distant bass from nearby clubs, just the occasional drone of a car and the drumming of the rain. The streets are narrow, a rat run of back alleys, wheeled bins piled high with crap. It smells rancid, and even though the dim lighting and the rain make it damned near impossible to get my bearings, I'm sure this isn't the way to the sea front. I haven't got a clue where I am or where the hell I'm going.

Shit, shit and more shit.

For the first time through this sorry mess I feel fear creeping up my spine. I'm out of my depth, and the tequila is wearing off fast. Way too fast.

My nerves are chattering worse than my teeth. I would kill for a cigarette, just to take the edge off, and as I turn the corner I may be in luck. A solitary figure is propped in a shadowy doorway. He's wearing a hoodie, so I can hardly see his face, not that I'm looking. I'm far too focused on the glow of the cigarette between his fingers.

"Hey," I say, smoothing back the wet hair from my face. "Could you

spare me a smoke?"

He stares at me, I can feel it, but I can't see his eyes in the shadows. He's big, much bigger than me. He smells of weed and stale body spray mixed with sweat, but right now none of that matters.

I launch into a monologue, telling him my name's Laine, and how I was out with a stupid friend who took my phone and keys with her when she left. I tell him it's my birthday, that I'm having the crappiest night of my life and he'd make it just a little bit better if he'd please give me a cigarette. I realise how stupid I sound, how weak my voice is. How weak I feel.

How alone I feel.

But I've felt alone for longer than I can remember, this shit's nothing new.

He hands me the cigarette from his fingers, and even though it makes me feel a bit icky, I take it from him.

"Thanks."

"Past your bedtime from the look of you," he grunts. His voice is thick and raspy, and it makes me feel uneasy.

I press myself against the wall, trying to hide from the downpour and protect the cigarette.

"Everyone says that." I take a long drag. "I'm eighteen. Perfectly legal, at least from today. *Yesterday*. It's not even my birthday anymore. Talk about celebrating in style, things can only get better, right?"

My stupid giggle and attempt at humour seem to go right over his head. He grunts again. *Perfectly legal*. I regret my choice of words.

I keep puffing away, looking at the floor, concentrating on nothing but the welcome rush of nicotine.

"All alone, then?" I can hear the sneer in his tone. He has an accent, a hint of cockney. It's gruff and deep and laced with the underbelly of this place.

I realise the fine hairs on the back of my neck are standing up and it's not from the cold. I realise I'm in a dark street with nobody around besides a man who makes me feel like a mouse in a trap.

I force a smile, gesture aimlessly at the road ahead. "My friend will be along for me soon," I lie. "She's coming back, such a ditz."

He laughs. "You just said she'd bailed. Make your mind up."

"Figure of speech," I lie again. "She'll be back... anytime now..."

"Sure she will." He takes a step towards me and I take a shuffle back. "You can drop the lost little girl shit."

"Sorry?" I keep my smile bright, even though my heart is thumping like a bastard.

"How much for the works?" I feel his eyes on me, all over me. He takes another step my way. "How much for a go on that cute little ass? Don't be shy now."

"But I'm not..." I drop the cigarette. "I'm not a..." My eyes are wide, but I still can't see his. "My friend's coming right now... she's on her way..."

He nudges the door behind him, and the stench of weed hits me. "Come up, get warm. I've got weed, or stronger shit, whatever you want. You'd like that, right? I bet you ain't so fucking innocent as you look." I can hear his smirk in his voice.

I shake my head. "She'll be here soon, and I'm really not... I shouldn't be here..."

"I bet you make a fucking fortune with that nice little girl shit."

"I'm not playing..." I move away from him, but back into one of the wheeled bins. Cardboard boxes fall to the floor and make me jump.

He laughs louder. "Come on, baby girl, don't be such a fucking tease." His voice is leery, drunk. "Bet you sound real fucking nice when you've got a nice hard cock in your snatch."

My back is pressed tight against the bin, and he's close, too close.

5

His breath is in my face. It stinks. *He* stinks. He smells musty and rank, like one of mum's old boyfriends… the window cleaner with the black tooth… the one who slipped his hand between my legs when we were watching Disney and never came over again…

"You want this… I want this…" His horrible laugh is right in my ear. I feel his lips on me. "You've got me all worked up, baby girl… you owe me for the smoke… you owe me now… what you gonna do about it?"

I look around, trying to catch sight of an exit, but there isn't one. He's too close, too big, and even if I made a break for it, where would I go?

"Don't…" I say. "Please…"

"Gonna warm you right up, make it feel real nice, if you're a good girl."

My chest feels tight, cold air hissing in my throat as I struggle to gulp it in. My heart is racing, but I feel disconnected, as though I'm not here, as though this is happening to someone else. I feel his breath on my neck, the warmth of his fingers as they slip inside my cardigan. I feel like I should be fighting, kicking and screaming and clawing at his face, but I'm so numb. So scared.

His thumb brushes my nipple and it shocks like electric.

"Knew you fucking wanted it," he grunts.

A strange sense of detachment washes over me, a sense of being sucked into a pit, where there is nothing, where everything is easy, where I can hide in the quiet place in my mind and pretend this is not me. It's his tongue against my ear that snaps me back to myself. It feels wet and hot.

"No," I say, and my voice sounds stronger this time. I'm wriggling, trying to bring my legs up, squirming away from his mouth.

"Chill the fuck out," he hisses, and my heart pounds in my ears.

The rumble of cars at the top of the street spurs me on, and I lash

out, catch him hard across the face. He swears and stumbles, touching his cheek for just long enough for me to kick out and make a run for it.

"HEY!" he calls. "GET THE FUCK BACK HERE!"

I hear his footsteps in the puddles behind me, the air in my lungs burning as my numb feet pound the street. I can feel him behind me but I daren't look back, just keep focused on the light at the top of the street, at the sound of a car heading closer. I see the headlights, blurry through the rain, and the danger behind me drives me straight into the road. I'm waving, jumping, throwing my arms above my head as I hear the screech of tyres. I close my eyes, a rabbit caught in the headlights.

I hear a car door slamming.

I jump a mile as a hand grips my elbow.

***

Nick

The girl jolts to life as I grip her arm, big blue eyes staring up at mine, lashes dripping. Her mouth is open, just a little. Her breath is misty.

She's young.

She's pretty.

And she's scared. Really fucking scared.

Footsteps pound the ground to my right, and I see him, the piece of shit waster.

The girl flinches, tugs away, but I keep a grip of her, place myself between her fragile little body and the dickhead chasing her.

He's wasted. Buzzing with some shit. Speed probably.

"Beat it," I say. "Fuck off back to where you came from."

He shrugs. "Just hanging with little Laine, bro. Ain't no problem here. C'mon, little girl."

Hell will freeze over before she goes anywhere with this piece of shit.

I smile at the loser. "I'm not your *bro*. Do yourself a favour and run the fuck along before there *is* a fucking problem here."

He looks me up and down, and even through the rain he clocks the cut of my suit. His eyes flick to the Mercedes, to the keys still clearly in the ignition.

"I wouldn't try it," I say. I take a step towards him, shoulders back and easy. I could take him and I know it. He's just another loser, another dreg from the cesspit of life, and I've seen plenty of those in my lifetime.

I glare at him, and beckon him forward, perfectly willing to put this piece of shit on the ground where he deserves, but he's backing away before I utter another word, druggie feet tripping over each other.

"Didn't mean nothing by it. Don't even know her... never met her..."

I don't bother watching him retreat. I've no need. Dickheads like him don't bother men like me.

I pull the girl closer, and she seems to snap back to herself. Her cardigan is sodden, hanging from her shoulders, and she's shivering.

"Laine?" I ask. "I'm Nick. Nick Lynch. You're safe now. Where do you need to go?"

"Newhaven..." she says, and her voice is as pretty as she is. "My friend... she pulled some guy... she has my keys, my money..."

"And where is your friend now?"

She shakes her head. "I don't know..."

"I'll take you home," I say, and my words are simple, obvious. I'm surprised when she follows me to the passenger door of the Merc and slips into the seat without hesitation, but she seems dazed somehow. Naïve, maybe. Maybe that's what got her into this mess in the first place. I suspect as much.

Young, naïve and vulnerable.

No way should she be out alone this late at night. No way should she be *here*, in this shithole part of Brighton. I feel the anger, at some unknown parents who should be worried sick, parents who should have taught her more fucking sense.

A father who should be driving around looking for his daughter, who should be protecting her from pieces of shit like that fucking waster back there.

I ignore the twitch in my jaw. Push aside *that* feeling.

She needs a ride home. Just a ride home.

She's not my problem, and she doesn't want to be.

I close the door after her and she buckles up oblivious. She's naïve. Definitely naïve.

But tonight she's safe. With me.

I'll keep her safe until I get her home.

She's staring right at me as I take the driver's side, still shivering, but she doesn't look so scared now.

I wait until the mist clears from the windscreen. The wipers give a rhythmic thump from the other side of the glass.

"I can't get in at home," she says quietly. "Not without my key…"

"What about your parents?"

She looks at the floor. "My mum's away."

"And your dad?"

"I don't have one."

"Your mum left you all alone?"

She nods. "She normally does."

My gut pangs. *No dad.*

I keep my voice steady. Warm and calm. "I can give you cash for a hotel. Take you wherever you need to go. Maybe a relative? An aunt or uncle? Neighbour?"

She's shaking her head. "I don't have… anyone…"

I feel the ache in my gut, stronger now. *Me neither.*

"You could call your phone, maybe she'll answer?"

She looks so embarrassed, shaking her head. "I turned it off… to save battery… it hardly had any battery…"

"Do you know your friend's number?"

Another shake of the head.

"How about Facebook? Social media?"

Her voice is so quiet. "Kelly Anne is um… she won't… she's with a guy, drunk…" She sighs. "She won't even give me a second thought… not tonight…"

Isn't that just the truth of it.

I put the car into gear. "Then you'd better stay with me until morning."

She doesn't even attempt to argue as I pull away.

***

Laine

I don't know where we're going. I don't know why I'm not scared.

My breath is steady now, and the air in the car is warm enough that my wet clothes don't feel so bad. My nerves are still on edge, I can feel them beneath the relief. The relief that I got away.

I stare at Nick, trying to figure out the guy who grabbed me in the rain and saved me. He saved me.

How could I ever be scared of a man who saved me?

He seems strong, Nick. He seems like the kind of man who could chase monsters away. His jaw is hard, and his nose looks like a Roman carving, and his hair is long enough to curl as it dries. He has heavy brows, serious eyes. He seems serious.

I feel safer than I've felt in a long, long time. Maybe I'm still drunk on tequila after all.

I feel so small and he feels so big.

"Don't you want to know where we're going?" he asks. His voice is nice. Deep. Strong, like the rest of him.

"Not really," I say. "Is it far?"

"No."

I shrug. "I don't really know my way around. I wouldn't know where we were if you told me, so it doesn't matter, does it?"

"I guess not, Laine, no."

I can't stop staring at him.

"Your friend doesn't sound like much of a friend."

"She's a crappy friend when she's drunk."

"That makes her a crappy friend, full stop." He glances in my direction. "A friend like that isn't worth having, Laine."

And he's right. I know he's right. But she's the only one I have. I don't want to tell him that, but I think he probably knows. He looks like he'd know a lot of things. He's a proper man. A serious man. A man who knows his way around the world.

11

"It's my birthday," I say. "My eighteenth. Yesterday. I didn't even want to go out."

"Eighteenth?" There's surprise in his voice. I hear that surprise from people all the time.

"Yeah, my eighteenth."

"I'm sure you've had much better birthday parties than this one."

But I haven't. They're normally shit. I don't want to tell him that either.

He turns into a petrol station and asks if I want anything. I don't.

He tells me to wait right there. I do.

I lose sight of him inside, and the nerves flutter in my belly. I feel like a kid again, a stupid kid. Maybe it's because I'm acting like one, buckled in tight in some stranger's car, trusting everything will be alright because he saw off some guy who was about to steal my V card in exchange for a crappy half-smoked cigarette.

That's what stupid kids do, right?

Stupid kids do stupid things.

I see him pay the cashier, I see him smile at her. He has a nice smile, the kind of smile that makes me feel like a silly girl with a crush. I'm sure I'd be crushing on a guy like Nick if I wasn't in such a ridiculously crap situation right now. The cashier's smiling right back, and I imagine he gets that a lot. You would if you were a guy who looked like him.

I pretend to be fiddling with my cardigan as he comes back to the car. He puts some bags in the back and slips back in without a word. I don't try to make conversation. I don't try to justify my stupid birthday decision-making processes.

We head out of Brighton. The roads turn to streets, and streets turn to lanes, and we're at big wooden gates at the foot of an incline. They open as the car pulls up to them, slide right to the side to let us pass.

Neat. The driveway is gravelled and opens up into a parking area, one of those nice ones where the gravel crunches under your feet. I bet it's that fancy pink stuff in the light.

His house is big. Really big.

Nicholas Lynch must be rich. I mean it's obvious he's rich. The car. But I wasn't thinking straight. I wasn't thinking straight enough to think about it.

He turns off the ignition and gets out. Opens my door for me.

"Home sweet home," he says. "I'll take you to Newhaven in the morning, we'll sort things out, Laine, don't worry."

I nod, and climb out. The gravel is the crunchy type, just like I thought. He grabs the bags from the back, and I look at the house. It's a barn conversion. Big windows line the lower floor. He locks the car and leads me to the front entrance. It's big and heavy with a wrought iron knocker. It creaks as he swings it open. I always wanted one of those when I was little – a big door knocker that would make a big thumping sound.

I'd have loved a house like this.

A proper home for a proper family.

I wonder if he has a family.

He gestures me inside and I feel awkward, my toes still squelchy from the rain. My pumps are soaked. I ditch them and go barefoot, and he doesn't seem to care that my hair is dripping down my back and onto his posh wooden floor. He leads the way through to a kitchen. It's huge and beamed and has one of those fancy range cookers, a granite island, too.

"What would you like to drink, Laine?"

"Just water, please." My voice sounds weak.

He takes a bottle from the fridge, pours it into a glass. The nice mineral stuff. His fingers touch mine as he hands it over, and they are

warm. Big.

"Thanks," I say. "For rescuing me. That guy… he was…"

"A waste of life. Scum."

I take a breath. "I'm such a complete idiot. Like Kelly Anne would ever stick around after a couple of tequilas." I laugh but it sounds pathetic. "What a dufus I am."

"She left you on your birthday. *She's* the *dufus*, Laine."

He slips off his coat, and I realise how tailored it is. He has a shirt on, white. It fits him so perfectly, like those people you see in expensive watch adverts. He could be one of those.

He rustles in one of the bags and pulls out a bunch of flowers, a cream cake, too. I watch mute. Like a fool. He digs around in a drawer and turns his back to me to block my view.

When he turns back around there is one of those little striped birthday candles stuck in the icing. It's lit, this tiny little flame flickering away.

I don't know why it makes me want to cry.

His eyes are so dark. It wasn't just the shadows in the car. He approaches and I'm not even watching the candle, I'm watching him.

"Happy birthday, Laine. Sorry, it's the best I could do. They didn't have much of a birthday selection at the petrol station."

The flowers are carnations. Red ones. The cake is chocolate. An eclair with that thick dark icing I love best.

It's the best birthday cake I've ever had. The thought pricks at my eyes and my throat feels scratchy. Ridiculous. *I'm* ridiculous.

Drunk, and high on adrenaline, and tired, and scared, and happy.

"Thanks," I say, like that could ever cut it.

But it does. It does cut it. He smiles like it's enough.

"Make a wish," he says.

And I do.

It's a stupid wish.

A crazy wish.

A wish I've been making every year for as long as I can remember.

I wish, I wish upon a star. I wish for my daddy, wherever you are.

I don't know where my daddy is. I wouldn't even know him if I saw him.

But right now, the guy who rescued me from the rain, the guy with the dark eyes, and the smattering of grey hair at his temples, and the shirt that looks like it came from an expensive watch advert. Right now, I wish *this* guy could be my daddy.

***

Chapter Two

Nick

The Maculinea Arion is the largest and rarest of the blue English butterflies. Little, blue-eyed Laine reminds me of one — fragile and delicate and inviting predators, with no idea of its own beauty.

I collect butterflies.

Not in a *put the lotion in the basket* style, just because I find them both fascinating and beautiful.

Unfortunately they're usually dead by the time I'm able to admire them now. Long gone are long summer days in the meadow, armed with a butterfly net and a *spotter guide* to British wildlife.

Laine's breath is a wisp, her eyes sparkling for a moment as she makes her birthday wish.

I want to ask what a girl like Laine wishes for, but I don't.

"You have a beautiful house," she says, and the colour is back in her cheeks.

"Thank you."

She asks me if I want to share her cake with her. I tell her it's all for her. She giggles as she gets cream down her chin, and I smile and laugh along with her, even though it makes my dick twitch.

It shouldn't, but it does.

She tells me she's a messy eater. Clumsy.

She says it's because she's one of those jittery people. Anxious.

I believe her.

It makes me want to grip her dithery fingers around my cock and jerk into her palm until I come.

It shouldn't, but it does.

I dig out a fluffy pink robe for her and tell her it's my daughter's. I take her to the bathroom and stand outside the door while she changes. She gives me her wet clothes in return, ready for the washer, and my pulse quickens at the sight of the bunch of little white knickers she's given me on the top of the bundle.

The robe dwarves her when she comes out onto the landing, skinny little legs so dainty underneath the swathes of pink towelling. Her hair is drying off, dripping at just the ends now, and her eyes are focused, sharp on mine.

She's ok here. She feels ok now. She tells me so. She thanks me again.

I give her a tour of the house and make idle conversation, show her the butterfly paintings in the hallway and the old net I had as a boy. She asks me how old I am and doesn't even apologise for it, just stares up at me until I give her an answer.

"Forty-two."

Too old for you.

I see the many questions behind her eyes and I wonder if she's interested in me or just naturally curious. She doesn't voice any of

them, but I ask about her.

Laine Seabourne. No father. No siblings. A mother who's off with her boyfriend, *Denny*. Laine is at college, studying childcare. Laine likes children.

I ask her why, and she says nobody has ever asked her that before.

I suspect there are a lot of things nobody has ever asked her before.

She sits in an armchair in my living room and pulls her legs up under her. Her fingers twiddle in her lap, fiddling with the dressing gown belt around her waist.

"Do you want children of your own, Laine?" I prompt. "Is that why?"

She shrugs. "I don't think that's why."

I wait. Listen to her breathe.

Her smile stills my heart. "I guess maybe it's because I get to give them the things I never had."

"The things you never had? You mean toys? Games?"

She shakes her head. "Time," she says. "Someone to play with. I think I enjoy it as much as they do." Her eyes glitter as she looks at me, and I wonder where she is in her mind. If she's playing teacups, or dolls, laughing as Barbie kisses Ken under the covers.

I wonder if she ever played that game.

"Didn't you have anyone to play with, Laine?"

"Sometimes," she says, "when Mum didn't have a boyfriend and wasn't at work. She played with me then. Sometimes."

"My daughter used to adore those little dolls that fit in your pocket. The ones with the rainbow hair, do you know them?"

She ponders, then shakes her head, and I realise how big the age difference is. Way before her time.

"What is your daughter's name?" she asks, and my heart prickles.

"Jane."

She smiles. "Thank Jane for her dressing gown. It's really cosy."

I nod, wonder if she'll ever find out that Jane never owned anything like the dressing gown Laine is wearing.

She won't find out. Of course she won't. I'll be taking her home tomorrow, making sure she gets in ok, and then I'll be leaving, nice knowing you. I'll wave her off and hope she has a nice life, glad to have been of service.

As Laine yawns and shoots me a grin, I know I'm lying to myself. She's comfortable here, with me, as though she's always been here. As though she belongs here.

"Time for bed," I say. "Up those wooden hills to Bedfordshire, young lady."

I'm smiling as I get to my feet, it seems so natural to hold out a hand to her. She takes it with wide eyes.

"Uncle Jack used to say that to me when I was little."

"Uncle Jack?"

"One of Mum's old boyfriends. One of the good guys." Her eyes drop. "One of the few."

My throat feels tight but I ignore it. "I'll show you to your room."

Your room.

She doesn't let go of my hand, not even when I've pulled her to her feet. She keeps it tight, her little fingers so small in mine. I walk her upstairs and intend to take her right to the end of the landing, to the regular guest room where the sheets are white and there is a TV, an ensuite and wardrobe and regular pictures of poppies and a seaside landscape. The boring room. I should take her there.

But I don't.

I reach Jane's room and my legs won't walk any further. I'm rooted to the spot, mouth dry as I press down the door handle.

Laine's eyes widen as I flick the light switch, and I know I'm doomed when she smiles.

"Oh wow! Wow!" she says, and she's taking it all in. The princess castle I made myself out of wood and silver paint. The rocking horse in the corner, the patchwork dollies on the shelf. I see her admire the little dressing table, the white wooden bed carved with hearts.

Sugar and spice and all things nice is stencilled on the wall above the bed.

"That's what little girls are made of," she says.

I nod. "Make yourself at home."

She squeezes my hand before she lets go. "Thanks, Nick. For everything. This is… beautiful…"

I squeeze hers back before I let her go.

"Sleep tight."

She sits herself on the bed and bounces. "Don't let the bedbugs bite."

She's smiling to herself as I close the door behind her.

***

Laine

This room is a fairytale paradise.

My heart hurts. It actually hurts.

I'm so jealous of the life Jane must have had, but mainly I'm grateful I get to enjoy it, even if it's just for one little night.

I sit at her dressing table and use her pretty mirror. I pull down her

dolls from the shelf one by one and brush their hair with her cute little princess comb. I look in all the rooms of her princess castle.

I wish I'd have had even one of these beautiful toys growing up.

I wish I'd have had a *sugar and spice and all things nice* message written above my bed.

But most of all I wish I'd had a dad like Nick.

Jane must've been so lucky.

I wonder how many times she played with the cute little Alice in Wonderland tea set at the bottom of the bed, whether she rode her rocking horse every single day or just took it for granted and left it sitting untouched. I wonder how long she's been gone from here. How old she is. What she looks like.

I snoop around a bit, but can't find any photographs of her.

There's one drawing, pinned behind the door. Nothing but a scribble really, a scribbled man with a smiley face.

DaDDy.

She must have been young when she drew that. Much too young to fit into the dressing gown I'm wearing.

My heart thumps in gratitude for her daddy. He saved me. Rescued me and gave me a birthday cake, kept me warm and dry and safe.

I hope he knows how grateful I am.

Maybe when I'm home I can offer him dinner, just something small, a little something to say thank you. Maybe I could cook for him. For *us*. Something nice…

The thought of Nick being in my house is like an ice water bath. Nick wouldn't belong there, amongst the cracked kitchen tiles and the fridge that doesn't really shut properly, not unless you kick it. Nick is opulent and stylish and classy. Nick is… Perfect.

My tummy flutters.

Nick is perfect.

I turn on the little white lamp on the bedside table and take off my dressing gown, feeling strangely young myself, naked in this little girl's room. I hang the dressing gown on the back of the door by the *DaDDy* picture.

I climb into Jane's bed and stare up at the ceiling, think about her lying here and knowing her daddy is just along the corridor, ready to keep her safe this day and tomorrow and the next day, and every single day until she's all grown up.

I wish that could have been me.

I think about Nick's firm grip on my arm when he rescued me from the road. I hear his voice as he told that horrible man to leave me alone. He was so strong, so powerful...

I think about his hand gripping mine.

I think about his hands...

I don't usually touch myself. Just every now and again, every so often. Kelly Anne laughs at me, says I'm a stupid prude because I've never even used a vibrator.

How can you never have used a vibrator? Christ, Laine, you're such a little kid!

I remember how she laughed when I told her I'd never used a tampon, only towels. I remember how horrified she'd looked when I told her I'd never put my fingers inside myself.

How can you not?! How can you even survive without sex, Laine?!

I survive just fine. I don't usually even think about it that much. I'm too busy with college, and keeping the house clean, and planning a future. Some kind of future.

I'm too busy trying to be a grown up, because my mother is pretty much incapable of being one. Always has been.

That's what I didn't tell Nick, when he asked why childcare. It's

because it's the only time I'm really happy, when I can disappear into a magical imaginary world with children and live there with them for a little while. When I can forget I'm a big girl who has to clean up after her mother because her mother's never been much of one for taking care of herself. When I can forget that I spent my evenings after school trying to cook myself dinner and do my homework and tidy the house up.

When I can forget about the noises coming through the wall from my mum's room every night and how they made me feel.

I sigh and it sounds loud in the room.

That should have been my birthday wish. *I wish I could live here forever.*

I think about it. Living here. Being Jane. And the thought makes me smile.

I think about Nick being my daddy, and making my breakfast in the morning and ruffling my hair.

I think about Nick holding my hand and telling me I'm a good girl. Kissing me on the head.

Kissing me.

I think about Nick's mouth.

His big hands.

I think about him touching me.

I think about him making the noises I heard through my bedroom wall.

I think about how it would feel. If it would hurt.

I rub my clit and it feels so naughty, touching myself in his daughter's bed while he sleeps down the corridor. It feels naughty and wrong, and maybe it's the combination of adrenaline and relief, but I can't stop, not even when I hear footsteps on the landing and realise he's not asleep. Not even when I reach that place where I breathe so

quickly I make little gasps, and my heart races, and my toes curl.

My breath is so loud when it's over.

I roll onto my side and pull my knees to my chest and realise that Jane's bed creaks.

I convince myself that Nick definitely won't have heard me. Definitely not, no way. Not one little chance. Not even one.

Until I hear his footsteps move away from the bedroom door.

Oh shit.

***

CHAPTER THREE

Nick

I tell myself I always leave the bathroom door open when I take my morning shower, that's one of the advantages of living alone. I tell myself I've always preferred the shower in the main bathroom — the one on the landing that opens directly across from Jane's door. I tell myself that Laine is asleep, that she's probably exhausted and I'll be long finished and dressed by the time she surfaces.

I wish to God I hadn't heard her last night. I wish I hadn't lingered, hadn't pressed my ear to her bedroom door to hear her exploring Jane's toys with curious fingers. Only those toys aren't Jane's toys. I never got a chance to give most of those beautiful toys to my little girl.

I wanted to make sure Laine went to sleep ok, that's what I tell myself. I wanted to be sure she wasn't still scared, wouldn't lie awake all night fretting over the piece of shit who tried to molest her in an

alleyway.

My cock definitely wasn't hard. It definitely didn't take all of my restraint not to jack myself off like a cheap pervert outside her door.

I definitely didn't want to hear her touching herself.

My shoulders feel tight until the hot water works its magic. The girl shouldn't even be here. This is reckless. Ridiculous.

I don't make stupid rash errors of judgement. That's something I learned from my father.

Every decision has consequences, he'd say. *Make sure you're well aware what they are before you subject yourself to them.*

He subjected me to enough *consequences* that I still bear the scars across my backside. Brutal, but fair, and he made me a better man for it. A smart man. A calculated man. A determined, responsible, powerful man.

Just like he was.

A man who doesn't pick up vulnerable young women and put them to bed in his little girl's room. If he wasn't already long in his grave, my father would tan my backside afresh for my stupidity. I smile to myself at his memory and lather on some bodywash. I scrub hard, working the suds into my skin as though they stand a chance of cleansing my impure urges.

I've worked hard to keep my impulses under control. Worked hard to express my desires in an *acceptable* way. Now really isn't the time to be thinking about them, not with temptation personified sleeping soundly across the landing. I shampoo my hair, working my fingers into my scalp, trying to get my head back in the game.

Breakfast. Laine will need breakfast. She'll need her clothes. She'll need taking back home, where she belongs.

Still, I can enjoy her just a little, just enough to get my blood pumping when I think back on her beautiful, innocent smile later this evening.

A bit of harmless fun never hurt anyone.

***

Laine

Jane's bed is really comfortable. Her room looks so warm and cosy as the light breaks through the gauzy curtains. I stretch out, kick back the sheets, relaxing quite happily until I remember with a thud that Nick heard me playing with myself last night.

Shit.

My heart races at the thought of facing him. How ungrateful can I possibly be? Taking advantage of his kind hospitality by playing with myself in his daughter's bedroom? In his daughter's pink bedsheets? Cringe doesn't even come close.

I bite my lip, think things through, and there's nothing else for it. I just need to get it over with. Smile and face him and hope he isn't too mad with me. I can't bear the thought of a man like Nick being mad with me. Disappointed in me.

I grab Jane's robe from the back of the door and trace my finger over the DaDDy writing on her picture. She's so lucky.

I make sure I'm wrapped up tight before I open the door, check myself in the dressing table mirror and smooth my wispy hair into some kind of order. I look so young in the morning light, in this room, as though I've regressed to being a little girl again.

The thought feels like warm marshmallows in my brain.

I hold my breath as I press down the door handle. Here we go. Now or never.

Maybe he isn't even up yet. Maybe he's already up and gone,

leaving my clothes in a pile with nothing but a *get out of my house, you dirty little bitch* message waiting for me.

I hope not.

I hear the water as soon as the door is ajar. The sound is much stronger than it is at my house, our shower is barely more than a trickle at best. I step out onto the landing and my tummy lurches as I see that the bathroom is opposite. The door is open, just a little bit. I can see a mirrored bathroom cabinet on the wall, all steamed up. A black towelling robe is in a heap on the floor. My breath hitches at the thought of him in there, the thought of him naked under the water.

For the first time in my life I don't want to be a virgin anymore. I want to be confident, like a sex vixen. One of those girls like Kelly Anne who can go after what she wants. If Kelly Anne were here she'd ditch the fluffy pink dressing gown and stalk in there naked. Flash him a smile and a *hello there* and climb straight in after him.

Hell, I'm nothing like Kelly Anne, and even if I were, a man like Nick isn't going to want a silly little girl like me. I wouldn't even know what I was doing.

He probably dates businesswomen types, older ladies with hot glasses and tight buns, and a wicked smile. Women who can talk politics with him over coffee and talk dirty with him between the sheets. The thought of Nick talking dirty makes my skin prickle.

I wonder again if he makes the kind of noises I've heard coming from Mum's bedroom.

I try to pull myself together, decide that it's probably better to go and wait in Jane's room until he's finished, but I don't. I'm in that strange place again, where everything feels surreal, and my feet are moving on their own, tiptoe steps so careful as I inch my way across the landing. Just a little further. I just want to see a little bit more…

I shouldn't. I really shouldn't. But I can't stop myself.

I don't want to stop myself.

I keep my eyes on the tiles as I edge closer. They are those expensive kind, like those spa hotels have. I went to one once for Kelly Anne's birthday, just for a swim, but I couldn't stop staring at everything. It was so beautiful, so grand. Nick's house is like that. He has one of those modern basins, one of the big ceramic bowls that sits on top of tiles, not like the tired old sink we have at mine. He has golden-brown towels over one of those fancy metal radiators. They match the colour of the bathroom perfectly. He's so stylish.

I think of those towels touching his skin, think of him rubbing himself down when he's finished, and my eyes creep further in, my toes edging closer to the doorway. I can feel the steam on my face.

It feels nice.

I shouldn't be doing this. I can't even believe I'm doing this.

I take a breath as my toes touch the tiles, eyes wide as I lean forward enough to peep around the door.

Insane. I'm insane.

But he left the door open… it was his mistake… maybe I didn't realise… maybe I wanted the toilet…

The sight of him makes my tummy flutter and lurch. He's got his back to me, his big fingers lathering shampoo into his hair. His shoulders are broad, and his back tapers into a slim waist. He's muscular… toned… I can see the definition in his back even through the steam.

Oh Lord, please don't let him see me…

He tips his head back to let the water rinse his hair, and his hands move over his body. I wish I could see the front of him. I wish I could see all of him.

He leans back, and his hands move lower. His perfect ass tightens, his thighs so tense, and I can see his arms, moving… and it feels so…

Dirty.

He's touching himself.

The wave of shock ripples through me, and it makes my brain pop … like the time I turned on the TV in the living room and it was on a channel it shouldn't be, playing one of Mum's boyfriend's dirty DVDs…

I'd closed my eyes instinctively, then watched it through splayed fingers knowing perfectly well I shouldn't. Knowing I shouldn't be tingling in private places, shouldn't want to touch myself at the sight of those big veiny dicks on screen.

They'd looked so big. Much bigger than I'd imagined.

Those men made the same noises I heard through my bedroom wall.

And Nick's making noises, too.

Quiet ones. Nothing but breath and grunts. I can barely hear him over the sound of the water but it's the most amazing thing I've ever heard.

My thighs clench tight, and it flutters there. I want to race back to Jane's bed and touch myself, but I can't, I can't stop watching. It seems to take forever, standing statue still as Nick's arm jerks and the water washes over him, but I don't care. I want it to take forever.

He braces a hand against the tiles and lowers his head, and his grunts are a bit louder now, his hips thrusting forward. He swears under his breath, and I know this is it, know he's about to come. I've seen it on the internet, I know how cocks look when men come. I wonder if Nick's looks just like that. My breath is so fast, but so shallow.

I watch it all. Watch him tense and thrust, soaking up the way his body looks, all the noises he makes.

When he's done, he relaxes, washes himself off like nothing's happened, and reality crashes in, the horror of knowing I've been spying on someone's most private moments. He turns off the water

quicker than I expect, and I'm sprung right out of my dazed state. I back away, clumsy this time, dash back across the landing to Jane's room and close the door behind me.

It closes too loud and I feel horrendous.

Embarrassment burns so hot.

I dive under the covers and pull them high over my head. Screw my eyes tight shut and try and calm my racing heart.

Shit.

Shit. Shit. Shit.

What the hell have I done?

I flinch as I hear a rap at the door, waiting for Nick to order me out of here, waiting for him to demand an explanation that I don't stand a hope in hell of giving.

The handle turns.

Slowly.

So slowly.

***

CHAPTER FOUR

Nick

I only caught a glimpse of her. A flash of pink as she darted from the bathroom, her presence confirmed by the sound of Jane's bedroom door closing across the landing. I don't know how long she'd been watching, but the thought of her blue eyes staring at my nakedness through steamy glass makes my balls tingle all over again.

I remind myself that this is unacceptable. I also remind myself that this is also going to be short-lived. A dirty flash in a very dangerous pan, but one I'll relive over and over in my fantasies when little Laine is long gone.

I rap at her door and give her a few seconds before turning the handle.

Her eyes are wide as I swing the door open and step inside, the bedcovers up to her chin, her pretty cheeks flushed pink. She looks guilty. Embarrassed. Gorgeous.

It suits her, and does nothing whatsoever to ease the temptation.

"Rise and shine, sleepyhead," I say, as though I haven't got any inkling she's just watched me whack one off in the shower. I cross the room with her eyes following me all the way, and her eyelashes flutter as I pull the curtains wide. Bright morning sunlight falls perfectly on her blonde hair. She looks so innocent, a little angel in a little girl's room. "I hope you slept well?"

She smiles a relieved smile, and she's so beautiful here, in this room. Her presence brings the place to life again.

She nods her pretty head. "I did. I slept really well. Thank you. Thank you so much for everything."

"Your clothes will be dry," I tell her, wishing I didn't have to. "Let's go down, get some breakfast. Are you hungry? You must be hungry, Laine."

She nods again, then throws back the covers, swinging her tiny feet out onto the floor. "Breakfast sounds really, really good."

She looks so warm and cosy wrapped in *Jane's* pink dressing gown. The urge to hug her is strong, to feel her tight against me. To hold someone again.

I take a breath. "Let's see what we can rustle up."

She follows me downstairs with bouncy steps, and her feet barely make a sound on the wooden floor as I lead her through to the kitchen. I pat one of the stools at the breakfast bar and she hitches herself up, adjusting her pink robe with a delightful little hint of self-consciousness that makes my mouth water.

I know I should show restraint and offer her a regular breakfast. Muesli or yoghurt, like I'll be having, maybe some toast with marmalade, but that perverse little thrill is tickling through me, and I veer away from sensibility enough to pull out the box of frosted puffs I picked up from the petrol station last night. I shake the box and hold it up for her to see, a grinning cartoon leprechaun gracing the packet.

"Do you like cereal, Laine? I thought you might like these."

36

How my dick twitches as her eyes light up. "I love frosted puffs! How did you know?!" she says.

I shrug. "A lucky guess."

"They're the ones with the marshmallow stars, aren't they? I begged my mum for those when I was little!"

Little. She looks so little. Perched on the stool.

I pour them into a bowl and pick her out one of my smallest spoons. A little spoon for a sweet little mouth.

She beams up at me as I place the bowl in front of her, as though I've just bought her a show pony, not a cheap box of cereal. I pour the milk, ask her to say when.

"When!" she giggles, and stirs the bowl with her spoon, watching the marshmallow stars drift around. They turn the milk pink.

I get us both an orange juice and sit myself down opposite her to eat my muesli. I watch everything. The way she scoops out just the right amount of frosted puffs with her stars. The way she closes her eyes as she crunches them. The innocent enjoyment in her smile.

I would happily watch little Laine Seabourne eat frosted puffs forever, and I feel a jab of resentment at the knowledge that I won't. It pains me that such a sweet, gracious girl has nobody waiting back at home to look after her. Nobody there to keep her safe.

But that's not my business, nor my problem.

"Tell me about Jane," she says, and it catches me off guard.

My breath catches in my throat. "About Jane? What do you want to know?"

She smiles. "Where is she? I guess she doesn't live here anymore?"

"No," I say. "Jane's long gone from here."

"All grown up," she grins, and it's the perfect opportunity for a subject change.

"So, how does it feel to be an official adult?" I ask. "Eighteen is a big milestone."

She shrugs. "I don't feel any different. I've kinda had to be an adult for a long time. Well, as much of an adult as I can be." Her smile doesn't mask her sadness, not quite. "I mean, it's my mum. She's just… she worked, when I was little. It was hard for her to take care of me. She tried."

Somehow I doubt that.

"So you had to take care of yourself?"

She nods, "Yeah. Nothing wrong with that though, right? It's good to be able to take care of yourself. I cook a mean toasted sandwich. Microwave meals? No problem." She giggles, but it sounds false. I don't answer and she sighs. "Jane is really lucky to have a dad like you. I'd have loved to have a dad like you."

"Thank you," I say, and the words almost stick in my throat.

"I mean it," she says. "Her room is amazing. The writing on her wall… her fairytale castle… all the toys she had…"

"Toys don't mean anything," I tell her. "It's love that matters."

Her spoon stops mid-air, and her eyes stare into mine. "I wouldn't know." She shakes her head, checks herself. "Sorry. Way too much information." She pulls a stupid face, tips her head to the side. "*Stop talking now, Laine.*" She dips her spoon back into the bowl and stirs the cereal.

"No," I say. "Don't stop talking. Not unless you want to, of course."

She fishes out a pink star. "These are really yummy."

I take the hint. "I'm glad you're enjoying it."

"So much," she says. "Really, really much."

She finishes up the bowl, and spoons up every last drop of milk. Then she waits. Watches me finish my muesli with a gentle smile on her face.

We sit in silence a for moment, and there's a feeling in me, a desperate urge to tell her she doesn't have to go home to an empty house, where nobody really cares about her. To tell her I like her. To tell her I want to take care of her, the way I wanted to take care of Jane all those years ago.

To tell her the truth.

I tell her nothing, just put our empty bowls in the sink and gather her clothes from the laundry room. She takes them from my arms, tells me thanks, and I force out the words I need to say.

"We'd better be getting you home."

***

Laine

The journey goes too quickly. The world zooms by outside the window and my heart thumps at the horror that this is it. Goodbye.

I really don't want this to be goodbye.

My palms are hot and clammy, and my fingers are fidgety. They twiddle around and around as I try to think of a way to make this last.

I just want to see him again.

My emotions are churned into a big messy ball in my stomach. It feels weird, uncomfortable, these feelings for Nick twisting and turning, so confused. I felt so safe in Jane's room, cocooned in this floaty bubble, like cotton candy at a spring fair. I felt so safe there, so safe in Nick's house, that I wanted to *be* Jane.

And I still want to be Jane now.

But I watched him. I watched him in the shower. I watched him

and I liked it. I thought about him touching me and I liked that too.

I like him.

I like him like *that*.

The combination feels icky. Weird.

Fluttery and weird.

I can't straighten it out and it won't go away, so I just keep staring out of the window and praying he'll let me see him again.

I can't bear the thought of never seeing him again.

He asks me for directions to Kelly Anne's house and I want to lie, tell him she lives far away, that I can't remember how to even get there, but I don't. I point him onto her estate in Newhaven, and he indicates onto her street.

I direct him into her parents' driveway and hold my breath, scared he'll say his goodbyes and disappear now I'm back on home turf. He doesn't.

He puts the car in neutral and says he'll wait for me.

I smile in relief.

"I'll be right back," I say. "Just a minute."

He nods, smiles, and I fumble with the door handle, trip over my nervy limbs as I bundle out of the car. I pull my cardigan around myself as I ring her doorbell, and I can smell his lavender fabric conditioner. I love the way it smells.

It's Kelly Anne's mum who answers the door. She takes my arm and welcomes me in, yelling to Kelly Anne upstairs to announce my arrival.

"Go on up," she says. "She's still in her pit."

"Thanks, Mrs Dean," I say.

She tuts at me. "It's Mary," she says. "How many times do I have to tell you it's Mary?" Her smile is kind and laced with that little bit of

pity I've grown used to.

I smile back at her then make my way upstairs. Kelly Anne's bedroom door is closed tight. I don't bother knocking, just let myself in and navigate the trail of dirty laundry until I'm at her bed.

"Kelly Anne?"

She groans, rolls over, and sleepy eyes barely focus on me.

"Kelly Anne, it's me."

"Laine? What are you doing here? What time is it?" She gropes for the phone on her bedside cabinet, checks the time and groans again. "Urgh, not even midday."

"You took my keys!" I snap, and all the fear from last night comes rushing back. "My phone, too! My purse *and* my ID! I was stuck out all night!"

She comes to her senses, props herself up on her elbow with a confused expression on her face. "What?"

I shake my head. "Jeez, Kels. You took everything! It was all in your bag!"

She raises her eyebrows. "No," she says. "It wasn't. It totally wasn't!"

I feel my jaw hit the floor, gawping as she roots around the floor for her handbag. She pulls out the contents. Lipstick and condoms and a load of crumpled receipts.

"But where…" I stammer. "What…"

"On the table!" she said. "You were in the toilet. I left your stuff right on the table for you! I even scribbled a note on a beer mat!"

"But there wasn't…" I think back to last night. To the horror of returning to my seat to find it occupied by other people, no Kelly Anne in sight. No Kelly Anne in the whole club.

"I left it with those guys…" she continues. "The ones we downed a shot with at the bar… they were right there, at the table next to ours…"

I can't hide the horror. "You left my stuff with a load of drunk guys and disappeared? You left my *money* and my *keys* and my *phone* with total strangers and bailed on me, on my own birthday?"

She covers her face with her hands. "Shit, Laine. I was wrecked. They seemed alright…"

"But they weren't alright. Clearly they weren't alright."

She stares at me, and her eyes are pink and hungover. "You got home though, right? No harm done."

"No. I didn't!"

She sits up in bed and I'm so angry, my nails are digging into my palms, thinking about what could've been, all because she was too busy getting down with some random guy. "So what happened?" she says. "Where did you go?!"

I try to start from the beginning, but the words won't come. I don't want them to. I don't want to tell her about Nick, or the guy in the alleyway, or being rescued. I don't want to tell her about Jane's room, and frosted puffs and watching him come in the shower.

It feels tickly, and raw. And private.

"So you don't have my stuff?" I say. "Not any of it?"

She groans. "Sorry. I'm really sorry, Laine. I pulled an asshole move."

At least she knows it.

I try not to let it upset me, just like always. Try not to take it to heart. Try not to comprehend the scale of the disaster on my hands now I'm in the cold light of day and still don't have any of my things. But it's hard. It's really hard.

"I'm gonna go," I say, and my voice is tickly.

"Go?! Go where?"

"Home…" I say. "I'll see if I can get in… through a window…"

She throws back the covers and starts gathering clothes from the floor. "I'll come with you."

"No!" I say, and my tone makes her stop in her tracks. "It's fine… you're still hungover, and I'm…"

"You're locked fucking out," she says, like I don't know that. "It's the least I can do."

And it is. It is the least she can do. But it's too late for that now, and I don't want her help, not with Nick outside.

I back away, heading for the door, tell her again that it's fine, that I'll cope, that she should get back to sleep.

She doesn't need all that much convincing. No real surprise there.

"Let me know you're alright, yeah?" she calls after me. "I've got so much to tell you about Harrison. That was his name, you know! Harrison! And he was so hot!"

Harrison.

That's the guy I have to thank for nearly losing my virginity to some asshole in a back alley.

I say goodbye to Mrs Dean on the way out, and do my best not to cry before I break the news to Nick.

***

CHAPTER FIVE

Nick

"All set?" I ask, and then I see the defeat in Laine's eyes.

She shakes her head, buckling herself into her seat with shaky fingers. Her voice comes out so weak, barely more than a whisper.

"Kelly Anne doesn't have my things. Not any of them. She left them, in the club."

"In the club?" I pull out my phone. "What was the name of the place? I'll call lost property."

Her dainty fingers reach out and land on my wrist, so gently. "There's no point..." she says. "She left them on the table... with some guys... when I was in the bathroom..."

My expression must speak volumes because her eyes widen as she continues. "She was drunk. She doesn't mean it. Kelly Anne is just..."

"Kelly Anne is a selfish fool," I say. "And you're so much better than friends like her, Laine."

She doesn't look like she believes me. Her eyes are sad and glassy, her cheeks pale. I put the car in gear, reverse out onto the street. "We'll go to yours," I say. "See what we can do."

"There may be a window open... upstairs... I may be able to climb through..."

There isn't a chance in hell I'm going to be letting her shimmy up some drainpipe, but I don't say that. Not yet.

Her estate leaves a lot to be desired. It's tired and cramped, with overgrown gardens and battered old cars in the street. Hers is a little white mid-terrace. The garden is neat but barren. The front door has chipped red paint, and as soon as I pull the car onto her driveway it's clear she won't need to be looking for an open window. The front door is already open, just enough to see into the dark hallway beyond.

Laine is out of the car in a flash, but I reach her before she makes it across the garden. I grip her elbow, pull her back to my side.

"Wait," I say, and my voice comes out harsher than I intend it to. "I'll go first."

I take a step forward, and as I nudge the door open I hear Laine's pained gasp behind me.

The place is a hovel. Nothing but a wasteland of empty beer cans and trash. There are fish and chips scattered all over the floor, a smear of tomato ketchup on the wall.

"Oh my God," she cries. "What the..."

I step on through to the living room, and it's in a worse state than the hallway. I find her keys on the cigarette-littered coffee table, and there's her ID, too. Laine's sweet face stares out from her college card, and there's everything they needed right there. Her address in plain lettering.

There's no sign of her phone or her money, of course.,

Laine busies herself around me, picking up empty bottles and cans through sniffles of pain, but it's a thankless task. The assholes

have clearly had a rare old time, no doubt thrilled at the hedonistic destruction of Laine's home.

She wipes her sniffles on her cardigan sleeve. "You can leave, Nick. Please leave. This is disgusting. Horrible… You don't need to be here…"

She clears another chip paper and underneath is a filthy used rubber. It's stained the fabric sofa underneath with a grotesque white smear.

I pull out my phone and dial the police, tell Laine exactly what I'm doing, but she shakes her head.

"What can the police do? They had a key! This is all my own fault! I should never have left Kelly Anne with my stuff…"

Her self-recrimination shocks me enough to cancel the call. "This is *not* your fault, Laine. Some dregs of society did this, some losers with no moral fibre, who exist just to wreck everything around them. *They* did this. Helped by your very considerate *friend*."

"But still, I should've known better! I should've known!"

"Don't touch that," I say as she tries to pick up the rubber in some greasy paper. "Don't touch anything. Not a single thing, Laine."

"But I have to…" she says. "I have to clean up!"

But she doesn't. She doesn't have to do a thing around this shithole.

"I mean it," I tell her. "Don't touch anything."

She stops moving, gives me a little nod.

"Wait right here."

She doesn't follow me as I survey the rest of the house, and I'm glad, because the place is completely destroyed.

The kitchen bore the worst of it, or so it appears until I reach the landing and see Laine's open bedroom door at the far end.

Her room is plain magnolia with some of the paint chipped away,

just like the rest of the place. Her bed is an old wooden thing, just a single, and her carpet is threadbare in places. What you can see of it, anyway.

It pains me to see how they've rampaged through her wardrobe, pains me further to find another used rubber in her bedsheets. They've taken her makeup and used it to scrawl obscenities over her dressing table mirror. The rest is trampled into the carpet. I pull a sweet white dress from her wastepaper basket, and it's been shredded, ripped almost clean in two. The rest of her clothes haven't fared much better, and my breath catches in my throat to see her torn knickers, cast from her chest of drawers and soiled in ways I don't even want to consider.

I hear her footsteps on the stairs, but I'm too late to stop her. She wails as she sees the carnage.

I grab for her as she launches herself towards the bed, but I'm not quick enough. She doesn't even see the grimy rubber, she's too focused on what's beyond.

And then I see it, too. A tattered bear, stuffing hanging from its dismembered limbs. She wrestles with her bedcovers until she finds its head, and she really does cry then, holding its broken pieces to her chest as she rocks back and forth.

I could kill the fuckers who did this to her.

She flinches when I lay a hand on her shoulder, and her words are broken. Choked.

"It's Ted," she sobs. "I've had him since I was a baby... I love him..."

"Shh," I say, and it's the most natural thing in the world to pull her into my arms. "I'll fix him, Laine."

Her delicate arms wrap around my waist, and she buries her face against my shirt. "Why did they do this? Why did they do this to Ted?"

"Because they're assholes who don't have anything better to do with their poxy lives."

Her sniffles are so sad. "I'm... I'm so glad you're here... thank

you…"

And I know this is it. I'm done for.

Her words are muffled against my chest. "I don't know how I'm going to tell Mum… she's going to be so mad…"

"You don't need to worry about that," I say. I take her cheeks and tilt her head up to mine, and her watery eyes are so beautiful. "Let's go now."

"Go where?"

"Home," I say simply. "Home to mine."

"But I can't… I have to stay… I have to fix this…"

I brush her tears away with my thumbs.

"You don't have to fix anything, Laine," I tell her. "Not anymore."

***

Laine

My heart hurts and I feel sick.

"You're so kind…"

He takes Ted from my arms and finds his missing leg. My poor, poor Ted. His battered body breaks my heart. My voice is all choked up as I ask Nick the question.

"Do you think you can save him?"

"I'll give it my very best shot," he tells me, and I believe him. He looks around my bedroom. "There's nothing else worth saving," he says. "I'm sorry, Laine, we'll have to get new."

"But I don't…" I cough to hide the embarrassment. "I don't have

any money… not enough… not even if I did have my purse…"

"You don't need to worry about that."

But I am. I am worried about that. He's done far too much already, and I tell him so. I tell him I can't take any more from him, that he hardly even knows me, but he waves his hand, won't hear any of it.

"I'll call a locksmith when we're back at home," he says. "Some cleaners, too. They'll salvage anything that can be saved." He runs a hand down my chipped paintwork. "I think we'll need a decorator, too. They've done a real number on the place, vile little cunts."

I gasp. It shocks me so much to hear him swear like that.

"Sorry," he says when he sees my open mouth.

But I like it. I like the way he sounds when he's angry. He sounds so strong… so fierce…

"I just can't believe there are people like this out there," he snaps. "Low-life scum."

"They didn't do all of this…" I admit. I point at the chipped paint. "That was already there."

"We'll get the place spruced up," he says. "I promise."

I smile, say yet another thank you, and I even try to sound convincing.

It's not that I'm not grateful, because I am. It's not that I'm not aware how lucky I am that I ran into the road and into Nick's path, because I'm very, very aware of that.

It's because I know that when we leave this house, and all the tattered broken things in here, I'm never ever going to want to come back.

He digs out a box from the garage. It's sad that one single box is going to be more than enough to contain the remnants of my life.

I'm relieved to find my college work intact above my wardrobe. I pack up my folders and text books, and place Ted on top, being careful with all his frayed pieces.

That's just about everything I can save. Everything I want to.

Everything that matters.

Nick carries it out to the car. He loads my measly possessions into the back and smiles as I slip into the passenger seat and buckle myself in. He closes the front door and locks it, and I wait in the car as he calls at the neighbours on either side.

He says nothing about what they tell him, and I've never much liked the neighbours anyway, so I don't ask.

I don't want to know what happened here. I already know enough.

"I still think we should call the police," he says as he reverses away from the house.

"No point," I reply. "They won't care anyway."

"Of course they'll care, Laine. They're the police. It's their job to care."

"And this is a dead end street. There's always crap going on around here. They'll probably think it was a party I had myself while my mum was away. A party that got out of hand, and now I'm trying to cover my tracks before Mum gets back."

"They won't think that."

"They will," I insist, and he doesn't argue. I guess he knows it too.

We head back towards Brighton, and the further away from Newhaven we get, the more relieved I feel. He parks up at a multi-storey in the middle of town, and I look at him curiously as he gestures I should follow him.

"You need things," he explains as we head for the exit. "New clothes. Toiletries. A phone."

"But I…" I grasp his wrist and he stops. "I can't take all this from

51

you. I just can't."

He sighs. "Laine, I've more than enough money. It's nice to have someone to spend it on."

I think of Jane. I think about all the people a man like Nick should have in his life. A wife maybe. Friends. Just… people.

It's on the tip of my tongue to say so, but his hands are on my shoulders before the words are out.

"Please, Laine. It's my pleasure. Allow me to enjoy it."

"Just a few bits…" I say. "Just to tide me over… and I'll pay you back, I promise."

"No," he says. "You won't."

He takes my hand, and his fingers are solid. He walks quickly, and I have to take two steps for every one of his. It makes me feel so alive, to be rushing along at Nick's side. I let the sensation wash over me.

He leads me into the first clothes shop we see, one of the lovely little boutiques on the front. Everything looks expensive, really expensive, but he doesn't seem to care. He heads for a section at the back, with loads of pretty pastel colours, and I'm pleased. It's where I'd have headed myself.

I baulk at the price tags, tell him it's all too much, but he won't hear any of it. He's gathering up clothes more quickly than I can look at them, pretty shades of pink, and bright whites, lovely purples and teals and pale blues. He's chosen the smallest size on the rack, and he's right.

"Choose whatever you want, Laine," he says. "Anything you like."

But he's already chosen everything I like. I tell him so and he smiles.

"Great minds," he says, and heads for the changing rooms. I follow him, a little lamb dancing along behind such a powerful man. Everyone is looking at us. At *him*.

The sales assistants are whispering. They beam as he shows them

the collection, and then they chivvy me along to an empty cubicle at the back.

He waits for me, and I feel so self-conscious, trying on such beautiful clothes under harsh lighting. My skin looks pasty and pale, my eyes look tired and my hair looks wispy and fine. But the clothes. They look gorgeous.

I show him a tight pink cami over a pair of white jeans, and he likes them. He tells me so.

I try floaty dresses over tights, and he likes those more. I do a little twirl for him and he claps his hands, smiles at me.

He fetches me a fluffy white cardigan and it feels so soft against my skin.

He fetches me a winter duffle coat that makes me gasp when I see the price.

He fetches me a scarf, and a cute winter hat with a pom-pom. Boots, too, and a sparkly pink pair of flats that make me feel like a little princess.

And then he makes me take everything, and I can't, I really can't. It brings tears to my eyes.

"My pleasure, Laine. *Mine*," he says, and I have no words for that. Nothing other than another *thank you*, and it always sounds so lame.

I'm still staring at the items in the basket when he piles more in. Nightdresses, and socks and packs of knickers. He hovers by the bras, and I realise he's waiting for me to tell him my size. I feel my cheeks burn as I pick out the very smallest one they do.

"I don't have... much... up top," I say, and try to make light of it.

"You say that like it's a bad thing."

I laugh a little. "Isn't it?"

"No," he says. "It isn't. You're perfect the way you are, don't you dare ever think otherwise."

My tummy flutters.

He thinks I'm perfect.

And I know it's probably just a figure of speech, know he's probably just being nice, saying things to make me feel better, but I wish he wasn't.

I wish he meant it.

I pick out some bras, just plain white with a bit of lace. It's what I usually wear, and I regret my decision for a moment, worried I've made a bad impression, that I should've chosen something more sexy, more… grown up.

"Anything else you want, Laine? Anything at all?"

I shake my head, manage a smile. "I think you've just about covered it. So many things… so many beautiful things…"

He seems so pleased.

I can't bear to watch as he pays. I stare at my pumps instead, anywhere but at the total balance as he hands over his card.

He carries the bags, and asks me if we should carry on shopping. He's worried, he says, worried that I won't have enough clothes for the time being.

He has no idea that he's already bought me more than I ever had in my wardrobe at home.

I tell him no, I tell him thank you, I tell him that he's already done more for me than I can ever repay, and he settles on toiletries, leads me around the beauty shop until I've placed everything I need in a trolley.

I hope he's forgotten about a phone, but he hasn't. Of course he hasn't.

It's the first time I really dig my heels in.

"Please," I say. "It's too much!"

"You have to have a phone, Laine," he insists. "How will I be able to

contact you otherwise? How will I know you're safe?"

If I'm safe.

I shrug. "I'll borrow Kelly Anne's, if I need to."

"Wrong answer," he says, and marches me straight inside the shop.

The phone he chooses is ridiculously superior to the one stolen from me. It makes me cry stupid tears again, and I feel so overwhelmed, my belly full of this churning *something*. I can't straighten it out.

"You can't…" I say, and he takes my hand, squeezes it tight until I look at him.

"Do you like the phone, Laine?"

"The phone is amazing…"

"Then it's yours, my treat."

"But I…"

He doesn't let go of my hand. "Laine, I want you to listen to me, can you do that?"

I nod. I could listen to him forever.

"Sometimes in life you have to let people take care of you. Sometimes you have to accept that people want to help, want to be there for you. Not people like Kelly Anne, who care only for themselves and their own selfish pursuits, people who *want* to treat you nicely. You deserve to be treated nicely, Laine. I don't think you really know what it's like to be cared for, not properly."

"My mum, she…" I'm ready with the excuses again, but he silences me with a sigh.

"I want to take care of you, Laine. Will you let me?"

Those flutters in my tummy again. I don't know what to say. I stare at him open-mouthed.

"If this is all too much, if you really don't want me to be there for

you, you only have to say. I'll book you into a hotel while the work is being done on your house. You can take the clothes, and the toiletries, and the phone, and I'll drop you there and make sure I keep my distance. You won't ever have to see me again, not if you don't want to. I can just be the kind stranger who helped you when you needed a friend. If that's what you want." He squeezes my hand again. "You only have to say the word."

I stare. Mute. This terrible panic in my heart, a feeling of dread at the thought of him dropping me at a hotel and walking away.

"Laine?" he prompts, and I find the words.

"No!" I say, and my cheeks are burning. "Please. That's not what I want. I want to stay with you. You're the best thing that's ever happened to me."

I slam my mouth closed, searing with embarrassment, but he doesn't seem to care. He doesn't seem to care at all.

"Phew," he says, and pretends to wipe the sweat from his brow. "You had me worried for a second there."

His eyes are kind and bright, and I see him afresh, all over again. He really is perfect. The most perfect man I've ever met.

"I had to check," he says. "I had to make sure I wasn't railroading you into something you didn't want."

"You're not," I tell him, and I just come right out and say it. "I can't believe this is real. I can't believe *you're* real. Things like this… they don't really happen… not for me…"

"Oh, it's real," he says, and his eyes twinkle. "Now, let's go and pay for that phone."

I don't argue with him this time.

***

CHAPTER SIX

Nick

The phone is in Laine's lap as we drive back to mine, her fingers tracing the edges as though she's trying to convince herself its real. She keeps looking my way. Fleeting little glances that melt my heart.

"Have you lived alone a long time?" she asks as we pull in through the gates.

I nod. "A while."

"Do you get lonely?"

"Not anymore." I meet her eyes as I park up on the gravel.

"I get lonely," she says. "*Got* lonely."

"Your mum goes away often?"

"All the time."

I ask her the question I've been putting off. The one that defies all my sensibilities.

"Do you have anyone, Laine? A boyfriend or someone special…"

She shakes her head and I feel a stupid rush of relief.

"Do *you*?"

"No," I say.

She nods.

We take her bags in from the car, and I come back for the box of her old belongings.

The new phone is quickly forgotten as she turns her attention back to Ted. She tries to push his stuffing back into his broken body, and once again I feel the strange weight of responsibility.

I like it. I like that feeling a lot.

I dig out a needle and thread from my utility drawer, and she hands him over without question and perches herself on the arm of the sofa as I get to work. Her eyes don't stray from my fingers as I attach a tatty old leg back at the tear. My stitches are small and careful, making sure I line up the seams just so.

"Wow, you can sew," she says, and I feel the gentle wash of relief as my work holds up to scrutiny. "You really can fix him," she says. "I knew you would. I knew it."

Her faith is like golden honey. Her smile is from the heart.

I fix Ted's legs, and his arms follow easily enough. I take a breath before I line up his head, and his glassy eyes stare up at me as I stitch him up so carefully.

"Good as new," I say as I hand him over.

"Better than new." She hugs him tight. "He's very grateful." She giggles. "And so am I."

I gather up the remnants of cotton and slip the needle back

through the reel, and her eyes are on me. Her expression is one of reverence, and it thrills me. Her smile is adoring.

She leans in before I get to my feet, and her soft lips touch my cheek.

"Thank you."

I fight the urge to pull her close and hold her. Fight the urge to feel her little body against mine.

"You're very welcome, Laine." I pat the bear's head. "And so is Ted." I gesture to the stairs. "I think we'd better get him settled in to his new home. He's had a long day."

"Home," she repeats, and it's barely more than a breath. "I think he's going to like it here…"

Her smile is so bright. The most beautiful smile in the world. "…I think we both are."

*   *   *

Laine

"You have a choice," he says as we get to the landing, and there's something heavy in his tone. Something that gives me nervous flutters. "About where you sleep."

My heart thumps at the thought of sleeping with him. In his room. In his bed.

But that's not what he means.

I can't help but feel a little disappointed.

"I thought Jane's room would help you relax," he says. "But there is another room if you would prefer. A guest room."

He opens the door at the end of the landing.

I step on through and it's nice in there. Nice and airy and all creams and whites. Nice and grown up.

And boring.

I get a horrible lurch in my belly at the thought of saying goodbye to Jane's beautiful room.

"And it's a choice?" I ask.

He nods.

"Jane's room," I say quickly. "I'd like to stay there please."

He smiles, and I see something pass across his features.

I wonder if I've made the wrong call. If I should have gone for the grown up room.

Maybe now he'll see me as a little girl who needs looking after, and part of me wants that. Part of me wants to be his little girl.

But another part doesn't.

Another part wants other things. Things that make me tingle.

Tingle down there.

We carry my things through to Jane's room, and he opens the wardrobe. It's empty.

"Make yourself at home," he says. "This room is yours, for as long as you want it."

I wonder again about Jane. Surely she visits? How will she feel to turn up at home and find some strange girl in her bed?

I don't want to ask, and I don't, just smile and start unpacking my new clothes, hanging them up so neatly on the hangers.

He stays while I do it, sits himself down on the bed and places Ted on my pillow.

"My bedroom is the one on the left," he says. "Just next door."

"Just through the wall."

"Yes."

I smile at him. "That's nice to know."

I place all my new underwear in the drawer, and put my college books on the bookshelf, and the room is beginning to feel a little bit more like mine.

I want to stay here all afternoon, forever, but Nick has other plans.

He cooks dinner while I sit at the table and tell him about my college studies. We eat at the dining table and he makes me eat all my carrots like a good girl.

"You need your vitamins," he tells me.

I help him load up the dishwasher and I ask him about his job.

He's an accountant, a partner in his firm. He says he's always liked numbers. He likes the order and the control. Likes the logic of it. Likes being able to make things add up.

He tells me he works Monday through Friday in an office in town, but that he'll be able to drop me at college and pick me up again.

I tell him I'll be able to walk, that his house isn't too far away from Brighton College, not really, but he insists.

I get those tingles again at the thought of him dropping me at the college gates and giving me a kiss goodbye.

"I'll make you a packed lunch," he says. "You'll have to let me know what you like in your sandwiches."

Nobody's ever made me sandwiches before.

I tell him so and he looks sad. It's that pity thing again, like Kelly Anne's mum, and I don't like it. I don't want a man like Nick to pity me. I want him to see I'm a woman, a proper woman, even if I don't want to be one. Even if I want to be the little girl who draws him DaDDy pictures and has a packed lunch.

"I can look after myself," I say. "I'm an adult now."

"You don't need to look after yourself. Not anymore, Laine."

"Still," I say. "I can."

"I'm sure you can."

But he doesn't look sure. He doesn't look sure at all.

He checks his watch and stretches his arms above his head. His shirt rides up, just enough to see the flat ridge of his stomach, and I remember him in the shower.

I remember how good it felt to watch him jerking off.

"Bed time," he says. "Early start in the morning."

He gets me a glass of water to take upstairs, and I follow up right behind him. All I can think about is that hard muscle under his shirt, and how it would feel against my skin. How it would feel to touch him. My cheeks warm at the thought.

I grab one of my new nightdresses and he gives me a towel. I wash myself in the same shower he used, and it gives me such a rush to put my fingers between my legs and rub myself in the same spot I watched him come.

It makes me come too. A shuddery one that makes me gasp and press a hand to the tiles for balance.

I wonder if his cum has been there. Right in that spot where my fingers are touching.

I wash quickly after that, wrap my hair in a towel and slip on the nightdress while my skin is still clammy.

The fabric is white and it clings. I catch sight of my nipples in the bathroom mirror, the dark circles so obvious. You can see my hair, too. The hair between my legs.

And I know right then and there exactly how much I like Nick in *that* way, because I've never wanted anyone to see me before, not like this.

Nobody except him.

But it feels naughty to want to be seen like this.

I move so slowly as I step out of the bathroom, listening for any sign of him. I hold my breath and close my eyes, ears straining to hear movement, and I'm so excited when I hear a door handle.

I gulp a little breath as he steps out onto the landing, and he doesn't see me straight away, he's too busy fastening his dressing gown belt.

He notices my bare feet first, and his eyes move up, up and up, so very slowly. So slowly that I feel a heat rush from my toes to my cheeks.

He swallows when his gaze reaches the darkness between my legs, and I feel so self-conscious, so much of a stupid kid.

Kelly Anne would cringe if she could see how awkward I am, but I'm doing my best. I lean against the doorframe and push my chest forwards, wishing I had some actual breasts to show him.

I can barely bring myself to look at him, but when I do I can't look away again.

His eyes are dark and his breath is fast. There's an edge to him that I haven't seen before, something heavy and brooding. It makes my tummy tickle.

For the tiniest second I believe he wants me. Wants me like *that*, and my heart jumps, jumps and races away.

"Thanks for the nightdress," I say. "It's really nice."

His voice comes out raspy. "It looks beautiful on you, Laine."

I've never wanted anything as badly as I want him to touch me right now.

"You should get to bed," he says. "Get a decent night's sleep."

I nod but don't move, and he comes closer.

I can smell him. Rich and musky.

A proper man.

He brushes by me on his way into the bathroom, and my nipples catch on his robe.

It sends sparks all the way down between my legs, and I press my thighs together, stare up at him as I gasp a little breath.

He stays so still, and so do I.

I can hear my heartbeat in my ears, and I can feel his breath against my forehead.

It's so easy to tip my face up to his, and I want it so much. I want him to kiss me so much.

"You need to get to bed," he says, and his voice is strained. "Right now, Laine."

I meet his eyes, and I want it. I want all of it.

I want him to be my first.

I want him to be the one.

His eyes are hooded and his jaw is tight, but he doesn't move, doesn't move a muscle.

"Please, Laine," he says, and there's a desperation to it. "Please go to bed… like a good girl."

Like a good girl.

I want that, too.

I want to be a good girl for Nick.

His fingers brush my arm and it makes me tremble.

"Go," he says and his voice is serious this time. "You need to go."

But I can't move an inch.

***

CHAPTER SEVEN

Nick

I want to shout at her. I want to lose my cool and push her away from me. Bark out orders that she needs to get herself to bed, where she belongs, safe under the covers and away from the lesser man inside me. The man who wants to tear that slip of a nightdress from those pretty little tits and devour her whole.

She's staring up at me, those doe eyes so wide and innocent. Only she's not innocent. Not right now.

It's clear what little Laine is thinking, what she's wanting.

"I'm not a…" she begins, and I close my eyes. "I'm not a… girl… I'm eighteen, Nick…"

"And I'm much too old for you. *Much* too old."

"But… but who says so?" Her voice is quiet and gentle. Her voice is perfect.

"I say so," I tell her simply and force myself to meet her eyes. "It wouldn't be right."

She nods, but she doesn't believe me. I'm not even sure I believe myself. Because here, on the landing, with this beautiful creature standing so close, with those sweet little nipples poking through flimsy fabric and her tight little pussy just begging to be taken, it feels more right than I dare to admit.

She looks so hurt. It's in the sag of her shoulders, the confidence of her stance fading into nothing. It only makes me want her more.

Her pretty eyes are glassy, and her pale little fingers are fidgeting, and I can feel her, the heat of her.

"I know I look young… and I know I act it, too… what with Ted and liking stupid cereals and not being able to get myself home at night… but I'm… I'm not… that's not who I am…"

"I like you as you are, Laine. I like you with Ted and I like you liking stupid cereals and needing someone. There's nothing wrong with being vulnerable, there's nothing wrong with needing help."

"But there is…" she whispers. "Because I like you… like *that.*"

I make myself say the right words. The *sane* words. "You've had a traumatic experience. It's easy to get confused, Laine. To believe you want something that maybe you don't."

She's shaking her head before I've finished. "I've never… I've never wanted… not ever." She takes a breath. "I've never liked anyone like *that.* Like *this.*"

The lesser man in me wants to believe her. The lesser man in me has all the justification he needs to ravage her delicate little body and make her mine.

But I don't.

"You don't know me," I say.

"I know enough…"

No. No she doesn't.

I shake my head, but she's not listening. Her fingers come up to

grip my arms, as though her touch has the power to defy my words and I catch the scent of her, the soap she used to wash, mixed with that divine aroma of crazy young hormones. I can't deny the eager twitch beneath my robe.

"I see you, Nick. I see how much you care for me, how you've taken care of me, how you rescued me. You make me feel safe, you make me feel wanted, you make me feel…" Her voice dries up.

"Make you feel what..?"

She takes a little breath.

"…How do I make you feel?"

Her fingers squeeze, and she smiles a sad smile, and my heart is hers. It's been hers since she stared up at me in the rain. It's been hers since she blew out her birthday candle.

"Loved," she whispers. "You make me feel loved. And I've never… had that… and I want to… show you…"

Show you how grateful I am.

I take her wrists, rub her knuckles with my thumbs as I ease them away from me. "You don't need to use sex that way, Laine. Love comes freely, it needs no reward. Never give yourself to someone because you feel you owe them something."

She looks so horrified.

"That's not what I meant… I wouldn't…" Her lip trembles and it's intoxicating. And I'm almost at breaking point, hovering on the edge of self-control as my fingers brush the ridge of her collarbone. "This is going so wrong…"

I'm about to slip the nightdress strap from her pale shoulder as she says the words.

"I'm a virgin, Nick. I'd never use sex to say thank you. Not ever."

A virgin.

Of course she is.

67

I'm freefalling. Lost to that primal force that wants to take her innocence and break it and make her mine. My balls tighten at the thought, cock twitching under my robe, my mouth watering at the thought of tasting her virgin pussy.

Her voice is breaking. Barely more than a whisper as she bares her soul.

"I want... wanted you to be my first..."

The girl is so naive. Naive and sweet and innocent. Totally unaware of the brutal urges of male flesh. It makes me want her so much more.

I watch my fingers back away from her nightdress strap. They move against the grain, gliding up to stroke her cheek.

"Someone special, Laine," I tell her. "Wait for that someone really special."

Two glistening tears track down her cheeks, but she smiles a sad smile. "I'm sorry... I've ruined everything..."

My hand slips to the back of her neck and I pull her to me, until I can feel the softness of her through my robe, the press of her face to my chest.

I wonder if she's playing with me. I wonder if she's a siren from the deep, calling out to me with the vulnerability in her song, and I'll be drowned, as all lusty sailors drown.

But I don't think so. I don't believe little Laine Seabourne knows how to play games.

"I'm so sorry," she cries, and I can feel her voice against me. "I thought you wanted me..."

She won't look at me.

If she looked at me, I wouldn't need to say the words that seal my doom.

I watch as my hand tugs the towel from her head and strokes her hair softly. And the words come, "I do want you."

My voice is laced with more than want. It's laced with need.

The need to consume.

To take.

To own.

I feel her stiffen in my arms, and it's too much. I snake an arm around her slender waist and pin her to me, and my fingers travel down, over the tight globes of her ass, and she's just as perky as I imagined.

I hitch her, and it's beyond doubt she really is a virgin, because she gasps as she feels the ridge of my cock against her belly. I circle my hips, and my robe works itself loose as she moves with me.

The sensation of flimsy satin between my stiff cock and her soft belly is such beautiful torture.

"This isn't about *want*," I hiss. "It's about what's *right*."

She's all breath and wriggling flesh, her flushed face tipping up to mine. She wraps her arms around my neck and presses tight, and her hips move, pin my cock to my stomach, where my balls ache and my dick wants to shoot its load all over her nightdress.

And then I push her away.

Firmly.

"Not here."

There's something in my tone I can't hold back, and she hears it. The nod of her head tells me everything, her eyes so eager to please.

"I need to shower," I say.

She nods again.

"I'll go to bed… I'll be… if you want…"

Oh, how I fucking want.

Laine

My legs are jittery as I cross the landing to the safety of Jane's room.

Shit. Shit, shit and total shit.

I want nothing more than to call Kelly Anne and tell her about my epic seduction fail. She'd laugh and tell me I'm a fool, and I'd have to laugh too, even though the thought of it is already burning me up, confessing my V status on his landing like some kind of stupid imbecile.

I don't even know what came over me, and maybe that means he's right, maybe it's some kind of trauma shit that's got me all worked up and acting weird.

Maybe that's why I'm a freak enough to want him to be my daddy one minute, and want him to be my lover the next.

How is he supposed to think I'm all grown up now, after I made such an epic fail of the whole sorry thing?

But I know that's not true. Because I felt him. And he was hard, hard and big. Big enough to make me nervous. Big enough to make it feel so real.

I turn Jane's little lamp on and look down at my belly, and he's left a mark, nothing but a faint little smear to show where his cock pressed against me. It makes the tingles between my legs come back so hard.

I want him.

Really want him.

I've never wanted to give myself to anyone before, not like I want to give myself to Nick.

I sit on Jane's bed and stare at the crack in the doorway, the door I've left slightly open.

I hear the water start up in the bathroom as I slip between Jane's sheets and pull them to my chin. It's so natural for my thighs to ease open, so easy for my fingers to slip down there and rub at my clit until I'm squirming all over again, and I don't even care anymore, don't care that this is his little girl's room and he's taking care of me, I don't care that it's disrespectful and stupid and not what I *should* do.

I don't care about any of those things, because I felt him, and I know he wants me. I know he wants me like *that*. And it's the most amazing feeling, to be wanted by a man like Nick. A real man.

A perfect man.

I wonder if he's going to be jerking off in there again, and the thought gives me flutters of panic that I won't be able to watch him.

I wonder if he's already convincing himself that he doesn't want me after all and I'm nothing but a dirty girl who needs to go home.

In my imagination, brave Laine leaps from the bed, whips off her nightdress and steps into the steaming shower, kneels before him, opens her mouth. I wonder what he tastes like.

I wonder if he thinks the same about me.

None of my wondering stops the dance of my fingers around my clit, none of it stops the ripples that rock through my body as I go over the edge and twitch and moan and struggle for breath.

Nothing stops the pounding of my heart as I realise the water's stopped in the bathroom.

I feel so small as he appears in the doorway, such a silly little thing as I hide under Jane's covers, my breath still quick from playing with myself. I hope he doesn't notice.

His hair is damp, just like mine feels on the pillow under my head, and he looks so nice.

His belt isn't tied tight this time, it's loose, barely wrapped around him. His robe shows a ridge of hard chest. A shadow of hair. And my heart is thudding all over again.

I wish I could see the rest of him.

He must know that, because I can't stop looking.

"We need to talk," he says. "But not tonight. Tonight is a school night."

I nod, and I don't even know why I'm nodding.

"We need to set some ground rules, Laine."

I keep nodding.

"We need to work out how this is going to be."

My head keeps on nodding, and I'm smiling a little too, because I think that sounds good. It has to be good, because he's not freaking out already and telling me to leave.

It has to be good, because his robe is hanging further open and he doesn't even care.

He doesn't care that I can see he's hard again.

That I can see he still wants me.

I can hardly breathe as he steps into the room.

I can hear my heart in my ears as he walks to the side of my bed and flicks off that little light.

My eyes struggle to adjust to the darkness, but they're too late to see him slip his dressing gown to the floor. I can only hear the rustle of fabric against skin.

And then the cold air as he pulls the covers aside.

The warmth as he slides in next to me.

The sadness as I realise he's wearing underwear, that the hardness of him feels so far away.

He pulls me close, my back to his chest, and it feels so right to wriggle into him.

His knees come up and hitch mine, his arm creeps around my waist and holds me tight, and his breath is on my neck. It tickles and my breasts tickle too and I want him to touch me so bad.

"We'll talk," he says. "Tomorrow."

"Okay," I say, and it sounds so dorky and pathetic.

"Ground rules, Laine. It's all about the ground rules."

I nod. Again.

Feel like a stupid kid. Again.

He's so big in this bed, so big next to me.

And this stupid little kid feels safe at least.

How I want his hand to move from my belly. Up or down, I don't care which.

But it doesn't move. Doesn't move an inch. Not even when I wriggle and squirm and feel his cock still hard against my ass.

My body doesn't feel like such a stupid kid at all. My body has a life of its own.

My body knows exactly what it wants to do.

But Nick won't give it to me.

He breathes into my hair and holds me tight, and finally he kisses my neck and it gives me tingles on top of tingles.

It takes me ages to calm down enough to go to sleep. His breathing is even and peaceful, his body so still as I squirm, and eventually I feel that, too.

I'm right on the edge of dreams as he whispers goodnight.

"Goodnight, Laine." Like it's the most natural thing in the world.

It feels natural.

Right.

This feels right.

And the words that come next feel too right to be wrong.

"*Goodnight, Daddy.*"

I hold my breath, scared he's going to pull away, ready with the stupid apologies and the excuses that I'm half-asleep and don't know what I'm saying.

But he doesn't.

He doesn't pull away.

I feel his cock against my ass all over again.

But he doesn't say a word.

***

CHAPTER EIGHT

Laine

I wake up on my own, and my heart does a little jump. A flip of panic at the thought he's left me, that he doesn't want me in the cold light of day.

I slip out of bed and grab my dressing gown, my feet quick on the stairs as I make my way down, and there he is, in the kitchen, and he's cooking.

He's already dressed, and he looks even more perfect in his suit this morning. His hair is slick and styled, and so dark that way that you can barely see the grey at his temples. His shirt is crisp and white, and he's so careful as he fries up eggs.

"Morning sleepyhead," he says, and he's smiling. His smile makes my tummy flutter. "I was just about to wake you. Food's up."

He flips the eggs onto a plate, and grabs some toast from the toaster. Bacon, too. I smell bacon.

It's the best smell in the world on a Monday morning.

I take a seat with a smile, say yet another thank you, and my fingers brush his as I take my plate from him. I feel it all the way up my arms.

"Are you all set for college?" he asks. "Anything else you need?"

He takes a seat opposite, tucks right in to his eggs like I didn't just call him Daddy last night. Like he didn't sleep in my bed with his big, hard cock against my ass.

"I'm all set," I say.

"Good." His eyes are so dark on mine. "I think we should make a start on those ground rules."

Rules.

I can handle rules.

I nod. "Ok."

"I'll be dropping you at college and picking you up at the end of the day. If there are any problems, you call me. If you're going to be late, you call me. If you need anything, you call me."

I nod. "Sure."

"We eat dinner together every evening. You do your college work here. If you need help with it, you ask me."

"Ok."

His eyes don't leave mine. "Do you have any obligations, Laine? Any jobs? Friends? Clubs you need to attend?"

I shake my head. "Just babysitting. Casually. Most weekends." I pause. "And Kelly Anne. Sometimes I hang out with her."

"There's no more need for babysitting, Laine. You'll have an allowance. It's better you concentrate on your studying."

I feel like I should argue, tell him he's done too much already, but there's something different about him this morning. Something so… authoritative.

I don't want to argue with him, so I don't.

And I like that I don't.

I like how it feels to have rules.

To have someone who cares the way he does.

"Ok," I say, and he smiles.

"Good girl." He tips his head. "How are your eggs?"

I've barely noticed them. "Perfect," I say, and it's true. They're just right. Just the right amount of runny.

I dip my toast in and they sure taste great.

Everything is great around Nick.

He slides my phone across the table. "I've saved my number in your contacts. You're on an unlimited plan."

"Thank you."

"I'll call you, at lunchtime. Just to check in on you."

I can't stop my goofy smile. "Thank you."

"There'll be other rules," he tells me. "But they aren't for now."

I nod. "Ok."

Ok. Everything really does feel ok.

Better than ok.

I feel all the words in my throat. Words about last night, about how good it felt to have him beside me. About how much I like him, how grateful I am, how he's the best thing ever, and I really mean it.

But they don't come out.

I just smile, like an idiot, and eat my breakfast.

He takes my plate when I'm done and loads it into the dishwasher with his.

"Get ready," he says. "We leave in fifteen minutes. We can't be late, Laine. I'm never late." He fastens up his cufflinks and slips on his suit

jacket from a hanger on the door, and I'm staring, gawping like a silly fool, until he raises an eyebrow. "Chop-chop," he says, but his eyes are sparkling. "You don't want to try my patience, sweet thing."

I don't try his patience, not even a bit. But there's a weird flutter between my legs at the thought.

***

Nick

She cradles her lunchbox in her lap, looking at it as though she's never had one before. Maybe she hasn't.

It pleases me to see her so taken aback by simple gestures. It's one of the things I love the most about Laine, the way everything is a wonder, everything is such a gift.

Spoiling Laine Seabourne brings me great pleasure.

Disciplining Laine Seabourne will easily bring me equal pleasure.

But I don't let myself consider that. Not yet.

Not before we've worked out the ground rules.

I pull up at the college and she looks so hesitant.

"All set?" I ask, and she nods. "I'll call you at lunch."

She nods again, but she doesn't move. "Thank you, for the ride."

"My pleasure," I tell her, and her little fingers grip the door catch before she changes her mind and leans in my direction.

Her lips brush my cheek for just a moment, but I feel the contact right the way through to my dick.

"See you later, Nick."

Nick.

That will have to change.

All in good time.

I watch her leave, her college bag thrown over her shoulder, her tiny frame wrapped up tight in her new coat. She's still holding her lunch as she makes her way to the entrance, and it fills me with a sense of satisfaction I've been missing for far too long.

It feels so good to have someone to take care of. Someone to care for.

Someone to love.

I'm about to pull away when I see a girl bound up the steps and grab hold of Laine's elbow. The girl has a mass of dark curls, a face full of makeup, and I know, instinctively, that this must be Kelly Anne. Laine's useless, selfish non-friend.

I see Laine shrug, and Kelly Anne is looking in my direction. She sees the car and says something, and Laine shrugs again before she carries on walking.

I wait until they're out of sight before I drive away.

I think it's time Kelly Anne was added to the ground rules.

I make a mental note of that for later.

***

Laine

"So? What the hell, Laine? Who's the Mercedes guy?"

Kelly Anne won't let up, and it's annoying. It makes me feel awkward and uneasy, like she's poking at something too private to be

shared.

"That's Nick," I tell her, like my answer stands a hope in hell of cutting it. "The guy who rescued me."

"*Nick*," she says. "And what's the deal with *Nick*?"

"He's looking after me." I try to outpace her but she's having none of it.

"Looking after you how?"

"I'm staying with him… while my house gets sorted… you know, the house you gave the key away to, the house that got totally invaded by a load of deadbeats from a shitty club while I was stranded in the rain."

She looks so horrified, and I'm glad.

I nod my head. "Yeah, Kels, *that* house."

"Jeez, Laine, I'm sorry. Mum saw Mrs Barnes from down your street yesterday, said your house got all fucked up. I'm a total fucking ass."

I don't reply in the affirmative, even though I probably should. "Nick's letting me stay at his. He sorted me out with some clothes. Brought me to college."

She stares at the lunchbox I'm still clutching to my chest. "Made you sandwiches…"

"Yeah, made me sandwiches."

She tugs at my elbow, but I don't let her see inside the box. "Don't you think that's a little…"

"A little what?"

She pulls a strange expression. "I dunno, a little *creepy*? Some random guy rescues you, buys you dresses and packs you a lunchbox. That's a bit creepy, no?"

I shrug. "He's not creepy. He's really nice."

"He could be a serial killer. Ted Bundy was a really nice guy, you know."

I laugh. "You've been watching too much CSI."

"Yeah, and you're really sweet. Too sweet. Like *take advantage of* sweet."

She'd be the one to know. If only I was bitch enough to point that out.

"I may not be worldly wise like you, but I'm not stupid. He's a nice guy. I like him."

And I guess I say like him with a little too much conviction, because her eyes widen and she gives me that look. The interrogation look.

"You *like* him?! Like *really* like him? Like want his dick *like* him?"

I sigh, back myself into the wall to let some people pass. "Yeah, I *like* him. I like him like *that*." And now I've said it I feel it all over again. The tickles and the flutters. That feeling of burning up. The memory of his body against mine.

Kelly Anne's mouth is open, and she looks so shocked. The most shocked I've ever seen her look.

"But he's… he's…"

"He's what?"

She struggles for words, which is totally unlike her. "He's like… old. Like an old guy."

"He's not an old guy." I laugh, and it sounds so high-pitched. "He's forty-two, that's not old."

"My dad's forty next summer, Laine. Forty. And *he's* an old guy." She sighs. "This Nick guy's old enough to be your dad, Laine. Isn't that weird?" She screws her face up. "*Gross.*"

The thought makes my heart pound, as though she'll know. Know the dirty thoughts I want to keep all to myself.

"I haven't really thought about it like that," I lie. "I just like him."

"And does he like you?" Her eyes are right on mine, and I can't lie. I don't know where to look. "Has he… tried anything?"

I shake my head. "No… it wasn't him… it was…"

"It was what?"

I feel my cheeks burning, and I put my finger over my lips until another crowd of students pass us by. "It was me…" I whisper. "I… I tried something…"

The grin spreads right across her face. "*You* tried something?! For real?"

I nod. "Yeah, and it was stupid, alright? I made a fool of myself."

She's trying not to laugh, I can tell. "I'm sure you didn't…"

"Yes," I say. "I totally did."

"And what did he do?" she's smiling so bright.

"He… he told me I didn't have to say thank you that way."

"And you don't, Laine. Using sex for that is totally skanky."

I don't even try and work out where Kelly Anne's rules on skanky sit. In her world it's ok to put it about to anyone who looks hot after a couple of tequilas, but clearly not to express gratitude that way. It's ok to ditch a friend to go running after a piece of random dick, but not ok to fancy someone old enough to be your dad.

"Well, he didn't take it."

"I'll bet he wanted to, though." She nudges me in the arm. "He must like you, Laine. Cute little blonde thing like you. I bet he's jerking off to the thought every five minutes. Dirty old man." Her laugh cuts right through me. "Seriously, though," she says, "you should come stay with me, not some random old guy."

The thought fills me with dread. "I'm good," I tell her. "I like it with Nick."

"Daddy Nick, making you sandwiches and buying you dresses. Very cute."

Daddy Nick. The thought has me burning up, and my heart keeps pounding and my mouth is all dry.

I barely register the fact she's still talking.

"So, where do you sleep? In his room? Please tell me it's not in his room…"

I shake my head. "In his daughter's room." I focus on a safer topic, tell her about Jane's lovely things, and the writing on her wall, and how great it feels there.

Kelly Anne doesn't look impressed, at all. Her eyes screw up and she looks at me like I'm some kind of crazy.

"You're staying in his kid daughter's room? With pink curtains and a mad hatter tea set?"

I shake my head. "It's not his kid daughter's room now. She's all grown up. She doesn't live there anymore."

Kelly tips her head to the side, and she's thinking. It makes me feel uneasy, and I'm glad class is starting soon.

"So… if she's not his kid daughter… then she's an adult now, right?"

I nod. "Yeah, I guess so. Probably moved away."

"So… if she's grown up… why is her room still like some kiddie shrine? I mean, where's all her teenage shit? Surely she'd have like *Backstreet Boys* posters up, or some other crap like that. Maybe some makeup… some grown-up kid shit…"

"Maybe she liked it that way… the way it was…" My answer is lame, and it's because I don't have one. Because I haven't even thought about it.

Haven't thought about the fact Jane's room is still like she's five or six years old, even though she doesn't live there anymore, hasn't lived

there for a long time.

"Maybe she lived with her mother..." I ponder aloud. "Maybe she didn't live in there... not all the time..."

"Still," Kelly Anne says. "She'd still have some grown-up shit, Laine. I mean, who wants a fairy castle when they're at high school?"

Me, I think, but I daren't say it.

"I'll ask him," I tell her. "About Jane. I'm sure maybe there's another room she had or something. Or maybe she didn't live there..."

Kelly Anne pulls a spooky face, waggles her fingers like a ghost. "Or maybe she didn't exist... oooooooh... maybe he's like the guy from Psycho and you'll find his dead mother in his cellar..."

That thought really does make me laugh. "You're an idiot," I tell her. "You really have been watching too much CSI."

I brush past her to make my way to class, and she follows, shrugs at me. "Tell me that when you realise he's some freaky pervert and you're running barefoot to my house as he chases you with his imaginary daughter's dildo or something."

"You're gross," I tell her, but I'm grinning.

"No," she says. "*You're* gross. *I'm* not the dirty little bitch with a creepy daddy fetish."

I laugh at her words but I'm not really sure what she means. I mean, she doesn't know Nick. Doesn't know how he saved me, how he cares for me. Doesn't know how safe I feel when I'm with him.

"He'd make a really good daddy," I say.

She rolls her eyes at me. "Tell him that while he takes your V card, Laine. That'll really get him off. Dirty old pervert."

I don't reply. I can't reply. In my mind, I'm sitting on his lap, my arms around his neck as he...

"Laine?"

I snap back to reality, and the heat in my face betrays me.

"I'm worried about you," she says.

But I'm not worried at all.

***

CHAPTER NINE

Nick

"*Morning, Mr Lynch.*"

A sea of the same old Monday morning greetings. I smile my usual smile, ask after people's weekends, and their kids, and their Saturday nights at the karaoke. I make my way through to my office with my usual take-out coffee and check my emails just like any other regular work morning. But it's different this morning. *I* feel so different this morning.

Jane stares out at me from the same old picture from the corner of my desk, grinning in the arms of her mother as they stare up at the camera. Stare at me. I touch the frame, a regular ritual, only this time my heart doesn't pang in quite the same way.

It's the loneliness. Or more specifically the lack of it.

A beautiful sense of relief washes over me as I discard my regular work routine and call my secretary through.

Penny looks great this morning. A new blouse, I think. She smiles

and scribbles down notes without even a hint of surprise as I instruct her to call in a cleaning team to Laine's property. I tell her they need to be able to handle hazardous waste, complete a thorough job from top to bottom. Decorators, I tell her. We'll need decorators when they're done.

Neutral colours. Maybe some fresh curtains to match. Yes, curtains to match.

New flooring, too. The place will need new flooring.

And a locksmith, to be safe.

I know I'm still lying to myself. Still maintaining the illusion that I'll ever want to see Laine move back into that place. It's a pretence that irks me, even the thought, but the girl needs to know she's in good hands, strong hands, hands that can save her from any of life's unfortunate situations.

And there's her mother to think about. If you can call the woman a mother in anything other than the biological context.

Anything else? Penny asks, and her smile catches my eye as her pen hovers so eagerly above her notepad. I notice the simple little pendant around her neck, sparking in the light. I notice the perfect pastel pink of her new blouse and the subtlety of her makeup.

"Yes," I say. "I'd like you to choose me some jewellery. As a gift for someone. Something tasteful." I pause. "Something you'd like, Penny. Something really special. I trust your judgement."

The compliment lights up her eyes.

"Sure thing, Mr Lynch," she says. "Do you have a budget in mind?"

I shake my head. "Something you'd choose for yourself, Penny. Budget is secondary."

She nods, dithers on the spot a little. I can tell she's plucking up the courage to pry, and I don't give her any cues, just stare at her with a professional smile on my face.

"Is she, um…" she finally begins.

"Is she..?"

"A *friend*?" she asks. "A relative?"

"Both," I tell her. "She's someone special."

She nods. "How old?" she asks, then checks herself. "So I know what style to go for, I mean."

"Eighteen. Just."

She looks at me as I say just, and I know she's wondering.

She doesn't ask any more questions, but I can say with certainty that my extra-curricular business will be the talk of the photocopier this morning.

That would usually bother me, but not today.

There isn't one single thing that will bother me today.

I call up my office calendar and mark myself as unavailable from four p.m. from this afternoon.

Sweet little Laine needs to get home safely from college.

And after all, it's a universal truth. A truth that everyone who is luckily enough to know it is blessed by.

A truth that I'm blessed with for the first time in years.

Family comes first.

In the meantime it's business as usual.

I ask Penny to bring in my nine a.m. client.

***

Laine

Nick calls me at lunch. It feels so strange to hear him on the phone. His voice is warm and deep, but there's a curtness to it. *Work Nick.*

I imagine him there, partner in some swanky accountancy firm. Solid handshakes and rich clients. I wonder if he has a secretary. I wonder if he has a big team of people hanging onto every word he says. He is the boss after all. Or one of them, at least.

Nick seems like a boss. He'd make a good boss.

Just like he'd make a good daddy.

And a good lover.

I get those crazy flutters again, butterflies in my tummy as I tell him I'm having a nice day, and my sandwiches were lovely. Ham and cheese. Posh ham, really thick cut. Not the watery stuff I buy for myself. I tell him my classes went well. That I've been working hard.

He sounds so pleased, and it makes me smile. When I hang up I'm grinning so hard I barely notice Kelly Anne gawping at me.

"New phone," she says, like it isn't obvious. "Quite a gift."

"I'm just borrowing it," I tell her, and that's how I see it, too.

She doesn't say anything, just gives me *that* look. That grossed-out look. But I don't care.

I meet Nick in the carpark at half past four, just where he left me. I see people staring at his Mercedes and it makes me feel strange, to be cared for by someone who wears a tailored suit, drives an expensive car and buys thick-sliced ham.

I've never had money before. Mum never even had a car. Not that it mattered.

I doubt she'd have driven me anywhere if she had.

Nick tells me he's had a good day at the office. Many meetings, he says, just an average Monday. I wish I knew what an average Monday was like for him. I wish I knew everything about him, but the questions in my head all sound stupid, and I really don't want to sound stupid.

"What are you thinking?" he asks, and there's that kind smile on his face again. He's interested. I know he's really interested, and that feels nice.

I shrug. "I was just wondering… about you…"

He laughs, and it's a lovely sound. "What are you wondering?"

"I dunno, just stuff." His smile makes me smile. "I just… don't know anything…"

"About me?" He stops at traffic lights and his hand reaches over to squeeze mine. "You'll get to know everything, Laine. Just give it time."

Everything. I like that thought.

"Ask me a question," he says. "Whatever you like."

So I do. I just ask him.

"Won't Jane mind me sleeping in her room?"

"No," he says. "She won't."

I look at him, but he's staring ahead. The lights turn green and he drives on.

"Will you tell her about me? That I'm staying, I mean."

"No," he says, and his smile is all gone.

I wish I'd never asked. I should've picked another question, something about the office or his house or his car. I stare out the window, and the route is already becoming familiar. The roads get quieter and there's the big tree I know means we're five minutes from home.

"I'll tell you about Jane," he says. "If that's what you want."

Kelly Anne's stupid paranoid speculations make me nervous, and I'm not so sure I do want to hear about Jane.

I feel his eyes on me for a moment. "Maybe talking about Jane will help you understand the ground rules."

"It will?"

He tips his head. "Maybe."

I don't say anything until he pulls through the gates and takes us up the driveway. I grab my college bag from the backseat, and he grabs his briefcase, and we're home again. *Home.*

He puts the kettle on and pours me a glass of juice, and I wonder if I've ever told him I don't like hot drinks all that much. He seems to know.

I sit at the table and watch him make his tea, just waiting. His eyes are so serious.

"Ground rules," he says, and I get a strange tickle between my legs.

He sits opposite me and I watch his hands around his mug. They're so big. So strong.

"What are they?" I ask. "The rules, I mean."

"I want to know you're safe, Laine, always. I'll need you to check in often. I don't want you taking rides in people's cars, I don't want you heading anywhere you don't know. Accidents happen that way," he says. "When people are careless."

"Careless," I repeat. "I don't take rides in many cars, Nick." I smile. "I don't have that many people that offer."

"A pretty young girl like you would have plenty of people offering to give you a ride, Laine. Maybe you just don't see it."

"I don't." I laugh. "I've never seen it. Kelly Anne is the popular one."

"Kelly Anne is reckless," he says. "Reckless and foolish, and selfish

on top. You're too good for her, Laine. I'd prefer it if you didn't let her drag you into any more situations."

I nod. "I'm not planning on it."

"Good girl," he says.

I meet his eyes, risk a smile. "Is that it? The ground rules? That I don't take rides in strange people's cars and don't hang out in clubs with Kelly Anne?"

"No," he tells me. "It's much wider than that."

That tickle again. It's something in his tone. Something so… strong.

"I want to take care of you," he says, and I can't stop that feeling between my legs. It makes my thighs clench together. "I want to look after you. I don't think anyone's ever looked after you, Laine. I want to be the first."

The first.

I want him to be my first. In every way.

"I can, um… take care of myself…" I offer. "You don't need to…"

"I want to," he says. "It gives me great pleasure."

And I don't know what this is. I don't know what we are, and I don't want to ask, and I do want to ask.

I do ask, but it comes out messy.

"You mean, like, a um. You mean like a… a guardian… or something like that?"

His eyes burn me and I can't look away. "Say it, Laine. Say what you mean."

My cheeks burn. "Like a, um. Like a dad?"

"Is that what you want?"

Yes.

I know that's what I want.

But I'm all icky again. All screwed up inside at the thought of wanting him like *that*. Wanting him the way that makes me all tickly between my legs.

"What?" he asks. "Tell me what you want."

I take a sip of juice and it's hard to swallow.

"You can tell me, Laine. You can tell me anything. We talk, about everything. That's another of the ground rules."

I nod, force down another sip of juice.

"This is a strange situation," he says. "For both of us. I was driving, just driving, and there you were, lost in the rain, needing someone. Just like I needed someone." He drinks some tea but his eyes are still on me. "Sometimes I think life has this way of putting people together in the most unlikely of circumstances."

"Like fate?"

He smiles. "I like to think of it as synchronicity."

"I believe in fate," I tell him. "I believe in horoscopes, too. I read mine every day."

"Maybe you should read mine," he says, and there's humour in it. "I'd love to know what fate has in store for us, Laine. I think it's good things."

"Me too," I say, and I mean it.

"So," he prompts. "What is it that you want?"

I shrug, gesture around me, to the beautiful room in his beautiful house. "*This*," I tell him. "*This everything*. It's... it's like a fairytale."

"Beauty and the beast?" He laughs.

"No!" I laugh with him. "Cinderella! I'm the scrubby servant girl and you're Prince Charming come to save me."

His eyes glitter. "I'm not all that charming," he says. "Not when you

get to know me."

But I don't believe him. I tell him so and he laughs again.

"Maybe this could be a fairytale, Laine," he says. "If we want it badly enough. Life is full of magic, I think, you just have to trust in it."

"I believe in magic," I say. "I haven't seen much of it, not until now, but I know it's out there."

"Maybe it's right here."

My heart daren't even hope. I feel it lurch, and it scares me how much I want this. It scares me how hard I'm falling, falling right into him, falling right into his life.

"I hope so." My voice is a whisper.

He holds out a hand and I take it across the table, and his fingers grip mine so tightly.

"Let me care for you, Laine. Will you do that?"

I nod. "I'd like that. Very much."

"And you'll stick to the ground rules? Let me keep you safe?"

"I'll stick to the ground rules," I say.

"Good girl." His smile gives me tingles on tingles, and my heart races.

I take a breath, stare at my hand in his. "And that's what you want? You want to take care of me? Like I'm…"

"Like you're my little girl?"

My cheeks must be like beetroot. I close my eyes as I nod.

"And what else do you want, Laine? What did you want on the landing last night? What did you want in bed last night as you wriggled and squirmed?"

I can't open my eyes. I just can't.

"You," I whisper. "I wanted *you*."

"Is that still what you want? Not out of gratitude, or because you think you should. None of that is necessary, Laine, I promise you."

I shake my head. "No... not because of that..." My heart is in my throat. "Just because... because I want it... because I like you..."

I hold my breath as I wait for him to answer, but his response shocks me enough to open my eyes.

"I need to tell you about Jane," he says.

"About Jane?"

"My rules can get... intense. I need you to understand why."

I nod, and my eyes are wide and focused. I'm pleased that he doesn't let go of my hand.

"Jane was my little girl," he says.

Was.

"I was young when I met her mother. Louisa was lost, just like you were. I found her sheltering under an awning during an autumn thunderstorm, upset because she'd argued with her piece of shit boyfriend. Jane was just a baby, fast asleep in her pushchair, none the wiser for her mother's predicament, thank God."

"So she wasn't..."

"Mine?" he says. "Not biologically, no. But she was mine in every way that matters. I was the man she called daddy. I was the man who read her bedtime stories and tucked her up in bed at night."

My eyes urge him to continue.

"I was young myself, relatively. Still climbing up the corporate ladder, coping with my father's death. This was our family home, I inherited it naturally, and it was lonely here before Louisa came, just as it was before you came."

"Did you bring her home, too?"

He smiles. "I did, yes. I brought her and little Jane home with me,

and made Louise cocoa while she dried off. I listened to her stories about her loser boyfriend and her sad life, and how she was so scared for tiny little Jane."

"You rescued her. You rescued both of them."

"Yes. Yes, I did. But she rescued me right back. Saved me from a life full of nothing but work and loneliness."

I take a breath. "She didn't grow up here, did she? Jane, I mean."

"She didn't grow up, Laine." He takes a breath. "She died when she was five. A car accident. Her and her mother alongside that sorry sack of shit I took her from." I see his eyes darken. "She left me a note before she went. He wanted to talk, she said, needed some help, she said. She didn't want him, but for some crazy reason that day she took our little girl and climbed into his car. Maybe she didn't realise he'd been drinking."

I feel the blood leave my face. "I'm so sorry."

"I should've been here," he says. "I was working late. Stupid client meeting."

"But you couldn't have known…"

"I didn't keep them safe," he tells me, and I feel the pain from him. I see it in his eyes, in the hunch of his shoulders, in the tightness in his voice. In his everything.

I squeeze his hand right back, as hard as I can. "I'll follow the ground rules," I tell him. "I'll stay safe, I promise." I feel so sad. So sad for that little girl with the pretty pink room. So sad for Nick, too. The whole thing feels so sad I can hardly draw breath.

"I just need you to be safe, Laine. I really need you to follow the rules."

I nod. "I will. Cross my heart."

He smiles such a sad smile. "I'll love you, Laine, if you'll let me. Hell knows, everyone needs someone to love them."

My heart hurts.

My heart knows that feeling.

I feel my eyes well up, and the tears spill, letting the sadness in my heart tip all the way over. "I'll love you, too, Nick. I'm so sorry about your little girl."

He runs his thumb over my knuckles and for that moment I'm sure I see his eyes are watery too.

And then he moves, takes a breath and gets to his feet, and he's in-control Nick again.

"Chicken for dinner," he tells me. "I hope you like chicken."

I tell him chicken sounds really good.

***

CHAPTER TEN

Nick

Laine tries to smile as though everything is A-ok as I prepare dinner, but she's thinking about Jane.

It's a phenomenon I'm familiar with, once people find out about such a loss. One that has long since found me avoiding almost all mentions of my little girl's name. It makes people feel awkward. Pity, sympathy… it's a fine line between the two.

I don't want either.

"It's ok. You can talk about her," I say as I peel the carrots.

She spins her empty juice class on the table top. "I just… I can't imagine the pain…"

"Hopefully you won't ever have to." The peeler works so methodically. I lift my eyes from the growing pile of carrot sticks. "It was a long time ago."

"Still," she says. "It's so horrible… it must've been…"

"Bad," I say. "It was bad."

I hope that will suffice. I have no desire to dredge up the long nights of misery, or the countless hours of therapy, or the emptiness Jane and Louisa's passing left in my life.

"I'm so sorry," she tells me, and I believe her. Those blue eyes glassy and melancholic, the sadness written all over her pretty face. "Is that why you rescued me? Because of Louisa?"

"No," I say. "I rescued you because of you."

She nods. "I'm so glad you did."

"So am I."

She smiles and it's both sad and breath-taking. "What did she look like?" she asks. "Jane, I mean."

I hesitate for just a moment, long enough to finish up a carrot and dig my wallet from my suit jacket. I flip it open and pull out the little picture. Jane's sweet little grin, her blonde pigtails. So happy. She looks so blissfully happy on that photo.

Laine takes it from me with dainty fingers.

"She was so pretty. Such a beautiful little girl."

"Yes, she was," I say. "A tiny blonde angel." I pause, staring at Laine staring at Jane. "Like you." She hands me the photo and I slip it back inside my wallet. "Louisa was blonde, too."

"Am I much like her?"

There's something in her tone — a hint of breathlessness, and that awkwardness she conveys so well. Her sweet self-consciousness is addictive.

I know she must be as confused as I am, spiralling around the same dilemma, just trying to ride the currents.

Lover or little girl.

Louisa or Jane.

I feel her brain ticking. I see it in her eyes, just as I feel it behind mine.

"You remind me of her sometimes. Just a fleeting memory here and there." I resume my peeling. "But you have an innocence Louisa didn't."

"Kelly Anne says I'm a prude, she says I'm a big baby. *Innocence is dumb stupid*, she says."

"It's a beautiful thing," I tell her. "Very endearing."

She smiles. "It is?"

"Very." And then I know it's time to lay it on the line. "Louisa wouldn't let me take care of her, not in the way she needed. Not in the way I should've."

Laine stares at me. "She wouldn't?"

I shake my head. "I should've set the ground rules earlier. It would've kept her safe." I laugh a sad laugh. "*Should've, could've.* Didn't."

"She didn't let you?"

"Louisa was reckless, right from the beginning. Rebellious. Addicted to the highs of her earlier life, even if she despised the lows. She'd say not, but it was in her soul, that sense of devilment."

"Rebellious," she repeats, then lets out a little laugh. "Then we're really not so similar at all. I barely even cross the road without a green light. Not unless Kelly Anne is involved."

"Kelly Anne needs someone to show her a firm hand, Laine. Teach the girl to be a lot more considerate of others. She'll get herself into trouble one day." I pause. "Only now she won't be dragging you into trouble's path along with her. I won't allow it."

I wait for a reaction, for any sign of backlash, but none comes.

"Thanks," she says. "For caring. It's nice."

I smile. "See if you still think that when you break one of the

ground rules."

Her expression doesn't change, and I'm sure the implication has sailed over her head. "I won't break them." She grins. "I'll be good."

"That's my girl." I finish up peeling the carrots. "You may well find me a little overprotective in time, Laine, but it'll be for your own good."

"I know," she says. "I trust you."

At least one of us does.

I start on the parsnips.

**

Laine

Nick can cook. But that figures.

Nick can do everything.

I eat up my chicken and vegetables, and it's all just perfect, just the way I like it. I never want to go back to microwave meals and pasta again.

I never want to go back to any of it.

My heart feels tender at the thought of poor little Jane. A horrible sickness, as though it's too big a pain to understand. And I suppose it is.

They say it's the worst pain on earth, losing a child, and my heart wants to reach out and hold Nick tight and never let him go.

I just don't understand why Louisa wouldn't want Nick to keep her safe. It's all I want.

That's a lie.

I want much more than that.

I want everything. Just like she had. Only more. I want all of it, every bit of his love, and his care, and his ground rules.

I'll give him all of my heart right back.

I eat up every bit of food on my plate and thank him for my meal. He tells me it's nice to have someone to cook for.

I tell him I'll cook for him one day. I tell him I can make a mean macaroni cheese. He tells me that'll be nice.

Somehow I don't think I'll be cooking for Nick anytime soon, but that's ok.

It's so easy to float around in my happy little bubble around him. So easy to be cared for. So easy to feel young and silly and small.

So easy to feel loved.

"Are you ok?" he asks. "You seem someplace else."

"Just thinking."

"Penny for them?"

I want to tell him that I love the salt and pepper at his temples, the strength in his jawline. I want to tell him that I love his gentle smile and the way he felt in bed last night.

I don't.

"I feel floaty. Like this is a dream."

"Me too," he says. "It's such a pleasure to find that life still has magic in it. It's been awhile."

"It feels like fate, doesn't it?"

He laughs. "Yes, Laine. It does. Maybe you'll have to read those horoscopes."

I clear up the dinner plates before he can stop me, and load them

into the dishwasher as he watches. I'm putting the cutlery into the tray as he steps up behind me, and his arms snake around my waist as he talks me through the washer settings.

Full cycle, half cycle, quick rinse.

I tell him I've got it, and press it to start.

I feel a pang of loss as he steps away.

He grabs his briefcase and sets out his laptop on the table. "Do you have homework? I've some reports to finish up if you want to work alongside me."

I don't have anything outstanding, but tell him I do. I gather up my text books and set myself up opposite him, then read over my notes from class, making myself out to be the diligent little student. It's not that far out. A swat, Kelly Anne calls me.

I listen to his fingers on the keyboard, taking care only to risk fleeting glances in his direction as he concentrates. His brow is firm. Serious. This must be work Nick. Professional Nick.

I scribble down notes alongside my notes, and it takes me a moment to realise he's staring at me.

"You have lovely handwriting," he comments. "Very neat."

My cheeks burn with a lovely warm feeling. "Thanks."

He reaches into his inside pocket and pulls out a pen. "Try this one. I find it writes well."

He's right, as always. The pen glides across the paper like a dream, glinting in the light like a silver bullet. I swirl my letters, making them just so, hoping he'll comment again when he surprises me with curveball.

"I'm too old for you," he says quietly.

My heart pounds. My throat dry and crackly. "Or *I'm* too young for *you*. That's what you really mean, isn't it?"

"No," he says. "It isn't. I'm thinking of you, not me." He sighs, and

I hate the sound. "I said we needed to talk about how things are going to be, and I've been thinking, Laine, I've been thinking a lot. I've been thinking here, looking at you right now, looking at the sweet girl with the pretty handwriting and the beautiful smile and wondering whether I can make her mine. Wondering whether I could be so selfish."

I can't bring myself to look at him, so I turn the pen over and over in my hands. "You're the best thing that's ever happened to me. You're the only one I want. How can that be selfish?"

"You're young," he says, and his voice is so calm. "You're beautiful, Laine. Kind and charming and gracious. You'll meet someone your own age, someone exciting, someone who'll knock you off your feet." His pause seems to take forever. "I'll still be here. Still be taking care of you, for as long as you need it, and even when you don't."

I have to summon up the courage to speak, forcing my crackled words out through my dry throat. "*You* excite me. *You* knock me off my feet. I can't even breathe sometimes… because I want… I want…"

"Laine…" he begins, but I shake my head.

"I watched you in the shower and I liked it. And last night, on the landing… when you…"

"When I lost control…"

"It felt amazing." I take a breath. "Please, Nick. Please don't stop this. Last night… I want that… I want more of that…"

He stares at me. "You've never been with a man before, Laine, How do you know you're ready?"

I laugh, but he doesn't. "I'm definitely ready. I'm the oldest virgin I know. A regular spinster."

"You've never come close, not with anyone?"

I shake my head. "There's never been anyone worth getting close to. Just idiots. Normally drunk idiots at that. The Kelly Anne effect."

"You've got a good head on your shoulders for such a sweet little

thing, Laine."

"I might not be cool and streetwise like Kelly is, but I know what I want, Nick. I know what's right, and what's not right. I know what's dumb, and what's safe and how to get through life without getting into too much trouble." My words stall as I remember him grabbing hold of me in the rain. "Well… usually… that night was…"

"Dangerous," he says. "It was dangerous."

"I should've been more careful." I try to keep my voice firm, try to sound so much more in control than I feel. "I'm usually more careful. I guess with Mum away, Kelly Anne was the only… I wanted to have fun…"

"It was your eighteenth. If there's a night for recklessness I imagine your eighteenth birthday is going to feature pretty highly on the list." He sighs. "It wasn't your fault, Laine."

"Even so," I say. "I was lucky."

"No," he tells me, and reaches across the table. I drop his lovely pen and take his hand, and those butterflies start their fluttering. "*I* was lucky."

"Fate," I whisper. "Like we said."

"And what do you think fate has in store for us, Laine?" His eyes are so fierce. Dark like treacle as they stare into mine.

"Everything." My voice is light, like air. "I think fate wants us to be everything."

"Everything?"

"Everything."

Tense. It's so tense. His eyes so serious and his jaw so hard. I can feel him thinking, feel him teetering on the edge, and I want to pull him over, pull him to me.

Please. Please, please, please.

I've never wanted anything so bad.

He squeezes my hand. "We'll take it slow," he says. "You can change your mind at any time, but be sure. Be sure you want this before we're both in too deep to get out."

"You mean we can… you'll be my…"

"Everything," he says. "If that's what you want."

I can't stop smiling. "I want that. I want everything. I won't change my mind. Not ever."

I worry I've overstepped the line, but he smiles back and my heart soars.

"This can't have any impact on the ground rules, Laine. How we are together, it doesn't make any difference, you'll still be in my care."

"It won't make a difference, I promise. I don't want it to, I like the ground rules."

His eyes sparkle, and he looks so strong again. There's that something primal underneath his cool, and I'm there on the landing again, in bed with his hardness against my ass again…

He pulls his hand from mine and closes his laptop.

"In that case, I think it's bedtime," he says. "Let's start starting slowly."

***

CHAPTER ELEVEN

Laine

My feet are bouncy as I follow Nick upstairs. He flashes a glance back at me, and his eyes are fierce, with a sexy kind of darkness that makes me feel like a clumsy kid.

I *am* a woman, I tell myself so. I'm eighteen after all. Totally ready for this. Totally ready for *him*.

If only the butterflies whirling round my tummy would believe me.

He gestures me on ahead at the landing, and I head for Jane's room before it occurs to me that maybe he won't want to… not in there… but he doesn't say a word, just follows me in and closes the door behind us.

And then he stands.

Staring.

Watching.

"What?" I giggle.

"I'm looking at you," he says, and my laughter dries up. "I love looking at you, Laine."

He examines me, up and down, taking in every single gawky part of me, and I try not to worry about my little breasts, or the weird-shaped birthmark on my thigh, or my bony knees. I try not to worry about whether I'll be good enough. "You're so very beautiful. You have no idea."

"Kelly Anne says I'm not sexy. She says I'm cute, like a doll, but not sexy. I don't really do sexy, though…" I admit, and I'm rambling. Nerves.

"I'm sick of hearing what that idiot Kelly Anne says," he says, and my eyes widen. "You're sexy *and* you're cute. You're everything she'd want to be if she wasn't putting it out to anyone who'll have her after a few tequilas."

I'm so aware of myself. So aware of the skinny jeans Nick bought me, and my baby pink cami and fluffy cardigan. So aware that I don't look dressed for this, despite his compliments and the warmth they give me inside. "Should I, um… change? Into something more…" I begin, but he shakes his head.

"No. You're perfect just as you are."

Perfect.

I want to feel perfect.

I want to *be* perfect… for him.

"I really don't know what I'm doing…" I take a breath. "I hope I'm not rubbish… I hope you're not…"

"Shh," he says, and my heart leaps as he moves towards me.

He's so tall, towering above me as he closes the distance. I can smell him. Woody and deep. I love the way he smells.

He tips his face up to mine and my breath comes in shallow little gulps.

"Relax," he whispers, and his head dips enough that his breath tickles my ear. His hands slide to my shoulders and squeeze, and it feels so right.

I feel the firmness of his chest through his shirt. The warmth of his fingers as they slip inside my cardigan and push it from my shoulders. I feel it crumple around my feet.

"My beautiful girl…" he whispers, and the husk in his tone makes my legs go quivery.

His breath is a warm rhythm, his lips pressing to my skin, and it makes me shiver wonderful shivers. I wrap my arms around his neck, the fine hairs prickling as he kisses so lightly along my jawline.

He pulls away, then pauses, eyes on mine, and I fidget, wet my lips, shuffle from foot to foot.

His eyes stay firm, right on target. My breath is so shallow and his is so steady.

He moves slowly. Lowers his head slowly.

And then his mouth lands right on mine.

The world stops moving. For that moment. Stops.

One long perfect moment.

And the butterflies go crazy.

His kiss is firm. Strong like him. Lips warm and soft.

His tongue pushes inside my mouth, and he lets out a groan, and I love that. I love the way it sounds. I love the way his tongue feels, too. Hot and just the right amount of wet. I love the way it moves around mine, the way he pushes so deep. I kiss him, like I think I should, my tongue twisting with his, my eyes closed tight as I take it all in. I'm making little noises, and my fingers tangle in his hair, and that's soft too.

He doesn't stop kissing me as he holds me tight and walks me backwards. My ankle catches on one of Jane's stuffed toys, and I

111

stumble, but he's got me. He holds me steady, guides me back a step at a time until I feel Jane's bed against my legs, and then he breaks the kiss. Pulls away with soft presses of his lips to mine.

I open my eyes and he's smiling. My lips feel puffy and tingly, and my cheeks burn hot as I smile back at him.

He runs his fingers through my hair, and I gasp as he pulls tight. He tips my head up, and I'm staring, staring at how strong he looks, how different he looks.

"You're such a good girl, Laine," he tells me, and my heart lifts for him. "I'm going to take care of you. That's what you want, isn't it?"

I nod, and the way my hair pulls in his fist catches my breath.

"You want to be my good girl, don't you?"

There's something in the way he says it. Something that makes me feel floaty.

"Yes." I nod again, and he pulls my hair tighter.

"A firm hand, Laine. That's what you need, isn't it? Someone to look after you. Someone to watch out for you. Someone to love you and nurture you."

"Yes… yes I do," I tell him, and that makes the tickles come harder.

"Don't be scared," he says, and there's that tone. That caring tone. "There's no need to be scared. No need to be nervous."

He lets go of my hair, and once again his fingers glide to my shoulders and squeeze. I feel the tension slipping away from me. His touch makes me feel so wanted, so loved.

I take a breath as his hands move down. Slowly. His fingers hook inside my cami and tug it down, and my stomach churns inside.

I feel so self-conscious in my plain bra, white and dull with just a little trim of lace. I wish I'd have picked something more raunchy, something more… *anything*, but the look in his eyes tells me he doesn't care. He doesn't care one bit.

The look in his eyes tells me he likes it.

His thumbs brush my nipples through the fabric, and I can't help but gasp; it feels so good I have to clench my thighs. He notices, and his smile is so bright and so dark at the same time.

"That's it," he whispers, and his thumbs stroke back and forth, tiny little movements that sends little sparkles all the way down to my clit. My nipples are hard, his thumbs catching, and I gasp again when he stops. I really don't want him to stop.

He lifts my top up and over my head. My hair swishes as the fabric pulls free, and I feel so exposed, standing before him with my little nipples poking out through my bra.

His hands are so hot on my bare stomach, skin tingling as his fingers sweep up my ribs. I find myself leaning back, rolling my shoulders to show more of myself than is really there, but his hands cup my little breasts, and nothing can hide how small they are. He thumbs again. Back and forth again. I'm clenching my thighs again, with quiet little gasps coming out with my breaths.

"Beautiful," he whispers, and his hands snake to my back. A flash of nerves as he unhooks the clasp, and my bra falls free. He drops it to the floor, and I look down at myself as he stares. My nipples are hard little peaks. They look so pink against my pale skin.

"You have such beautiful breasts, Laine. Beautiful."

I love the way he sounds so… mature.

In control. He sounds so in control.

"Thanks," I say, and I'm biting my lip as he rolls my little tits in his fingers, squeezing flesh that is barely there, tugging at nipples that send crazy sparks right through me.

He groans, and it's so horny I can feel it in my pussy. "Such pretty little tits, Laine. Sweet little nipples, so pink. They're perfect. I knew they'd be perfect."

I make a little squeak that I hope sounds grateful.

"Look," he says, and I do. I stare down at him playing with my nipples, and his hands seem so big, his fingers so strong as they pinch and pluck and flick at me. "Divine," he says. "You're simply divine, little Laine."

He tugs at them again and my clit sparks so crazily that I think I could come. Right here, right now, still in my jeans with nothing but his hands on my tits. My clit's fluttering so hard I'm clenching my thighs, over and over, rocking my hips to press myself against the denim seam.

"Good girl," he says. "Tell me that feels good."

I nod. "It feels really good."

He presses his knee to my thighs and I gasp as he makes me part them. He hitches me onto him, his thigh hot and firm between mine, and his hand grips my ass, encourages me to grind myself as his other hand presses to my ribs, coaxes me to arch my back.

Unsteady. I feel unsteady. But it feels too good to care.

I rub myself against Nick's thigh as my little tits stand proud for him. His breath is in my face, hot and steady as he presses my nipple and circles, and it feels so good I'm not nervous anymore. I moan as he twists and pinches, and I'm asking for more, asking for harder, and I don't even know what I want, I just want more.

He hitches me tighter against him, and I feel him. Feel his hardness against my belly. I rub myself faster, pressing myself tight, hoping he likes the way it feels, hoping he feels horny like I do. And he must, because his breathing gets faster, and his fingers get rougher, squeezing at my tit until I suck in breath.

"Yes…" I grip at his shoulders for leverage. "Please…"

"That's my good girl," he growls. "My sweet little horny girl."

I can't stop. Rubbing myself against him so fast. The denim of my jeans straining and the ridge of his dick feeling so big against my tummy.

"I'm gonna…" I begin, but I can't finish. I don't think I can say it. "I think I'm gonna…"

"Come," he says. "Come for me like a good girl, Laine. Come for me!"

And I do.

My clit does that fluttery thing that makes me gasp in breath, and I'm clenching and making little noises and rubbing so hard.

I'm humping Nick's leg like I'm on heat, and he wants it. I feel his dick tensing, pressing so hard.

He pinches my nipples, one after the other and I squeal for more, and then a tremor runs through me.

I shudder and squeak and rub and cry out, and I've never orgasmed like this. Never so hard.

He groans, and his hand is clammy against my back, his breath hot against my face as I slump against him, trying to gather my breath. Trying to gather my scattered thoughts.

"Good girl," he rasps, and I love it. I love it when he calls me that.

My heart is racing so fast I start giggling.

"That was amazing," I tell him. "Thank you. Wow, just… wow."

I'm smiling as I meet his eyes, and his are still burning, still fierce.

"That was barely the beginning, sweet Laine," he says, and his fingers reach for the button on my jeans.

***

CHAPTER TWELVE

Nick

My beautiful girl's eyes as so wide as I unbutton her jeans. Her cheeks flushed and her breath short as I pull down the zipper and slide the denim down her legs.

Her knickers are perfect. Plain white cotton, understated and innocent. *She's* perfect.

She steps out of the jeans so gracefully, and she still has her socks on, fluffy and pink and cute enough to make my cock twitch.

I drop to my knees, my face so close to her sweet pussy, hidden by knickers that are damp, and my breath lands right where I know she's so tender. Dainty fingers brush my scalp, twist in my hair, and she murmurs.

"Show me," I whisper, and my hands grip her pale thighs so firmly,

coaxing her until she shifts her legs apart.

Her skin is clammy on the inside of her thighs. I smile at the sweetest little birthmark. Not far below her pussy. It's almost like a heart.

I can see the promise of hair through the cotton, darker than the perfect blonde on her head, and it takes every scrap of restraint not to tear those knickers down and gorge on her sweet little cunt.

But slowly. Softly.

Gently.

I press my nose to the damp cotton and breathe in deep, and she smells divine. My sigh of pleasure tells her so, and her fingers tighten on my scalp.

"*Nick…*" she whispers before her voice trails off.

That will have to stop.

But not now.

Not this moment.

She tenses as I press my lips to her through the fabric. Whimpers as I rub my nose up and down, over the hard little clit I know is so horny for me. I taste her wetness, my tongue pushing at her through damp cotton, and I hold her tight, my hands on her firm little ass, squeezing and stroking as I lap at her knickers.

"Ah…" she whispers. "That's… *ah…*"

I suck at her. Grip her knickers in my teeth and tug, then suck some more.

She's squirmy in my hands, breathless again, letting out the little murmurs I love so much. I ease her thighs further apart, and she presses her pussy to my mouth like such a greedy little girl.

Yes. She's a greedy little girl.

My greedy little girl.

My cock fucking loves that.

I hook the elastic and peel her knickers down so slowly. She closes her legs as I slide them over her ankles, and she's nervous again, shielding her most delicate treasure.

I stare up at her until she meets my eyes, and then I shake my head.

"No," I say. "Never hide yourself from me. I want to see you."

She gives me a little nod, but her thighs stay closed.

"Everything, Laine," I tell her, and my voice is firm. "Show me that beautiful pussy."

She takes a deep breath and shuffles her feet wide, her sweet young slit glistening pink and perfect.

"Stunning," I tell her. "You're absolutely stunning, Laine. So sweet." I lean in and touch my tongue to her naked flesh, and she's soft and wet and delicious. I flick my tongue a little and she gasps a shuddery breath. "You taste divine, Laine. Absolutely divine."

"I do?" she says and I smile up at her innocence.

I tease my fingers up the inside of her thighs. So softly, I brush the delicate petals and spread them wide until she's raw and exposed. Her clit is a glorious bud, swollen and ripe, paddling in her excitement and begging to be sucked.

I blow a warm breath on her and she squirms. Tugs at my hair.

"Nick... please..."

Her head is tipped back, and I know her eyes are closed. I know she'll be screwing them shut as I run the point of my tongue along her slit and fasten my mouth so tightly on her puffy little mound. I stare up at her as I suck, and she's gasping so delightfully that I can't help palming my cock through my trousers.

Her fine nest of dark blonde hair tickles my nose. Her scent is the most heavenly nectar, hitting me right in the temples as my tongue probes to find her innocence. I daren't push in too far. Daren't spoil

I lower my face and taste her. Push my tongue inside just a little, just enough.

"I'm ready," she whispers. "If you want to…"

"Oh, I want to," I say. "But there's so much to do, Laine. So many pleasures to show you."

I grip her clit between my fingers, and she cries out as I suck it into my mouth. I suck so carefully, bringing up the pressure as she squirms, that little bud swelling in my mouth as her pussy clenches.

She drops her knees, and her fluffy heels dig into the bed, raising her up to grind back at me. I snake my arms under her ass and hold her tight, and her hands are in my hair, tugging as she begs me for harder. She whimpers like good little girl, asking so nicely, and I suck. Hard. Suck until she's panting, suck until her fingers are digging into my scalp and her feet are thrashing against the covers.

I suck until she cries out, loud, and my sweet little Laine swears.

"Fuck… *fuck, fuck, fuck…*"

I suck until she's crested, until she's holding her breath and her body is tense, wired tight as she unravels. And then she relaxes, lets all the tension out in one long sigh.

She jumps as I tap her pussy.

Just a light tap. A warning shot. Enough to make her startle.

"Potty mouth," I growl. "Dirty little girl."

Her eyes are so wide as she stares at me, unsure whether I'm serious or not. I see the worry play across her lips.

"Are you a dirty little girl, Laine?"

She bites her lip. Shakes her head, so unsure.

So innocent.

"I think you're a dirty little girl." I smile a dirty smile, and I can't control the beast. I can't fight the dark urges that want to consume her,

soil her, corrupt her, break her and make her mine.

All mine.

"I like…" she begins.

"What? What do you like?"

She pauses, her eyes sparkling so beautifully, her pussy still clenching and glistening. "I like… everything… I want… I want to be good…"

"You're going to be my good little dirty girl, are you?"

She nods. "I'll be whatever you want me to be…"

Oh fuck.

My cock jerks, my balls tight enough to blow.

She must notice my grimace, because her eyes travel down, over my creased shirt to the bulge between my legs.

She licks her lips, and her eyes flash with a dirty kind of devilment that takes my breath.

Dirty innocence. It's the most intoxicating kind.

"Can I see?" she asks, in the sweetest voice. "Can I see you?" She raises herself on her elbows, and she's smiling. "Please…"

I kneel up, my fingers working down my shirt buttons, but she moves like a quick little mouse, her fingers pushing mine out of the way.

They're shaking as she unbuttons my shirt.

Her cheeks are rosy as she slips it from my shoulders.

Her little fingers run down my chest, pressing against the ridges.

"You're so… firm…" she says.

"I like to keep fit," I tell her.

She nods, and her eyes meet mine for a moment as she brushes my nipple.

"You can touch me," I say. "Touch me however you want."

Her hands gain confidence, stroking and prodding and pinching. "You're amazing…" she whispers. "You're everything…"

I quiet her with my mouth, my lips pressing to hers before my tongue pushes inside. I tip her backwards and follow her, and her fingers snake instinctively to my belt.

I unbuckle for her, and pull out my cock, kissing her hard as I wrap her sweet little fingers around my shaft. I move her hands, up and down, nice and slowly.

"Like that," I groan into her mouth. "Just like that."

"I want to see it," she whispers. "Please…"

I press a hand to her ribs as I lift myself from her. Adjust her thighs so I can see her pretty cunt as her fingers work my dick. And she stares at my cock with wide-eyed wonder.

"It's big…" she says. "It feels so nice."

"It feels a lot nicer like this," I say, and press the head against her slit. She sucks in her breath but I smile, slide it up to her clit. I rub my cock against her wet little bud, and her palms press to my thighs.

I reach for her, my hand slipping behind her head to take her hair, supporting her weight so firmly.

"Look," I grunt. "Look how hard I am for your sweet little pussy."

"Do it," she whispers.

Back and forth I brush my swollen fucking cock, over that sensitive little nub until she's panting all over again.

"I need to come," I tell her.

"Please… yes…"

"Come with me…" I drop her to her back and lower myself back in position. My belly presses to hers, and her pretty little nipples feel so sweet against my chest.

"I can't…" she whispers. "I'm so… fluttery…"

"You can," I tell her. "I promise you, you can." I pause. "And you will. Again, Laine. Come for me again."

I rub, back and forth, my dick pinned between my stomach and her pussy, grinding hard, taking so much fucking care not to spear that tight little cunt and fill her up with my cum.

She wraps her legs around my waist and moves as I move. Her hands wrap around my neck and hold tight, eyes closed and mouth open as she gasps and moans and whimpers.

"I'm gonna come all over your sweet little pussy, Laine."

"Yes…" she whispers. "Oh God, please… please, Nick…"

"Don't call me that," I growl, and I'm on the edge, right on the fucking edge.

"What shall I call you?" she asks, and I hear it in her voice, I hear she's thinking it, too.

It's in the little tremor, the sweet little hint of lust.

My breath is erratic, my cock pulsing as my balls tighten, ready to fucking blow. And I say it. I just fucking say it.

"Call me Daddy," I growl. "You can call me Daddy."

She tenses, shudders, writhes against me.

She likes it.

I knew she would.

A moaning, squirming, delicious little angel.

I thrust, pin her hard, unloading my cum all over her tender little cunt, and she's right there with me, whimpering little squeals into my ear.

I collapse onto her, dick slick with my cum as it smears between us, and I feel her heartbeat against mine, so fast.

Her fingers play with my hair, her mouth to my ear. I hear her breathing. Her breath so fast.

She kisses me, her lips pressing so gently to my temple.

"Thank you... Daddy."

***

CHAPTER THIRTEEN

Nick

She's so small in my arms. Her dainty little limbs holding me so tight. Her hair smells of apples, nestled under my chin as she snuggles under the bedcovers.

Her breathing is so even. A sweet calmness I've not seen in her before.

I guess three orgasms do that to a girl.

The beauty of this... this tenderness I feel with her beside me, goes someway to disarming the uneasy feeling in my stomach.

I've crossed a line. A big line. A line that makes me feel like a depraved excuse for a man.

And yet little Laine rests so peacefully, presses her body to mine with a devotion I've missed for so long.

She moves, and her hair tickles my chin. I feel her eyes on me in the darkness.

"You should be asleep," I tell her.

She sighs, and her little fingers stroke my arm. "Was I ok?"

I hold her tight. "You were more than ok, you were perfect."

She presses her lips to my collarbone. "You were perfect, too. You were everything."

Everything.

I've waited so long to be someone's everything.

I stretch out my legs, her toes rub against them and she sighs a sweet little sigh, and there's a part of me that wants to draw a line under this murky half-light between lover and father. A part of me that wants to pick her up and carry her through to my actual bedroom, with its big double bed, and its neutral decor, and close the door to Jane's room forever.

But I can't. The need to love her as the captivating, innocent little soul in pink is far too strong.

"Daddy…" she whispers. "I've always wanted a daddy."

A thrill of lust ripples through me, more than enough to counter my self-revulsion.

"I'll take care of you, like any good father should," I tell her. "You're safe here. You'll always be safe with me."

"I know," she says. "I like it… I like calling you that…"

I'm done for, my dick twitching at the desire to hear her say it again.

"*Daddy.*" Her voice is nothing but a breath. "Can I really call you that?"

"Do you want to?"

She nods, and I feel her smile against my skin. "Yes." She pulls away enough to search my face in the darkness. "As long as that doesn't… change anything… because I want… I want…"

"Shh," I say and brush my fingers through her hair. "*Nothing* will change anything. We're just…" I struggle to find the words. "Different, Laine. We're different. Two people who find what they need in each other. In the most… unusual of circumstances."

"Fate," she says, and it sounds so simple. "It's fate. I know it is."

"Fate," I repeat.

I want to believe her. I find no fate in numbers, or balancing books, or managing a business. I find nothing but cold hard logic behind every aspect of my life. Apart from in her. In her beautiful innocence. In her wide eyes, and her sweet smile.

I find fate here, in my arms.

"Daddy," she whispers so softly.

"Yes, sweetheart?"

"When will we… you know…"

I seek out her lips and kiss her gently. Tasting her breath. Breathing in apples and innocence.

"Soon," I say. "Now go to sleep, like a good girl."

She wriggles against me with a contented sigh.

"Yes, Daddy."

***

Laine

I wake to an empty bed, but it smells of him, all woody and dark and musky. I pull the covers to my nose and breathe him in, and there's a thrill all the way to my toes.

Daddy. Daddy Nick. And he loves me.

I can still feel his hands on me, and his mouth, the way it felt so good. The way *he* made it feel. He makes *everything* feel good.

"Wake up, sleepyhead! Breakfast's up!"

His voice is so loud from downstairs. It makes me smile, and I can't move fast enough, jumping out of bed and throwing on my dressing gown. I laugh to myself as I realise I've still got silly socks on. Toasty feet.

He's dressed for work as I join him at the table, and he's smiling his serious smile again, looking so dapper and fine with his hair so slick.

"Bacon and eggs. Yummy." I take my knife and fork, and his eyes burn my cheeks.

"You look cute," he says. "Like a dishevelled little elf."

I brush my hair down with my fingers. "You look like a Rolex advert."

He laughs. "I do, do I?"

I nod. "I like it." I can't stop looking at him, and my clit feels tingly, wanting more, wanting his cock inside me for the first time, wanting to stay in bed and do it all over again, all day long.

He must be able to tell, because his smile turns dark, his eyes stern.

"Eat your breakfast all up, little Laine," he says, "never any waste in this household."

"Ok." I smile as I cut up my bacon, and he's still staring as I take a swig of juice.

"Ok, what?"

My heart flutters. And I don't know. I don't know if I've got it right but I say it anyway.

"Ok, Daddy."

I got it right. His smile tells me so.

"That's my good girl," he says.

It feels the best thing in the world to be his good girl.

I eat my breakfast all up, just like Daddy wants me to.

***

Laine

He kisses me on the head outside the college gates, and part of me is disappointed, wanting to feel his tongue in my mouth and his hands in my hair.

"I'll call you at lunchtime," he tells me. "And I'll pick you up at the usual time. Don't be late."

I nod. "I won't. Thanks, Daddy. See you later."

It still feels so weird, still gives me this tingle in my belly every time I say it.

I'm grinning as Kelly Anne catches me up in the corridor, lost in my own little world as she shunts into my back.

"Hey!" she says. "Earth to Laine! I've been yelling after you right through the fucking car park."

I shrug. "Didn't hear you, sorry."

She groans. "Your head's too busy floating away after the creepy old guy. Urgh, I saw him kiss you." She pulls a face at the lunchbox in my arms. "What you got today? Human spleen on wholemeal?"

"Don't be stupid."

She laughs, like it's funny. "He's a bit *Hannibal*, don't you think? *My sweet Clarice... are the lambs still screaming...*" She groans again, an over the top sound that grates at me. "Just because he drives a flash car

and buys you shit doesn't mean he's not a Class-A weirdo."

It's her expression, one I haven't seen on her before. I guess it's a little in the shift of her feet, too. The way she shuffles, the scowl beneath her stupid jokes.

She's jealous.

And I can't believe it, I can't believe Kelly Anne is actually jealous of me.

"He's nice," I tell her. "He's really nice."

"Nice and creepy…"

"Nice and *nice*. Kind and strong and considerate and thoughtful and loving."

"Loving?" She raises her eyebrows. "Oh my God, did he… *touch* you? Major gross-out."

I'm a bad person, I must be, because I want to tell her everything, want to tell her all about how amazing he made me feel, and how good he was and how much he loves me. I want to tell her that it's fate, and I love him and he loves me, and he's going to take care of me, hold me tight, and make my lunch every day, and take my virginity and it's going to be everything I ever wanted, not some crappy fumble with Kyle Vickers behind the school bins like hers was.

"Laine…" she prompts. "Did he..? Are you..? Jeez, don't tell me you finally ditched the V-card?"

I tug her elbow and pull her to the side of the corridor. "No. Not yet. But I will."

She rolls her eyes. "For real? You and Hannibal? So many hot guys out there and you pick the creepy old dude. Daddy issues much?"

My cheeks are on fire. My whole body feels on fire.

"That's what this is, right?" She laughs. "Daddy issues." She pretends to suck her thumb and I get an icky rush of butterflies. "*Ooh, Daddy, that feels so nice, Daddy. I'll be a good little girl, Daddy.*"

"Stop it," I say. "It was nice. The whole thing was amazing."

She props herself against the wall, acts like the big, cool girl. "The whole thing? So spill, oh virginal one, what is *the whole thing*?"

She's ruining it. My only friend, my only confidante, even if she's always been a shit one, and she's ruining it.

"Forget it," I mumble, and make to move past her.

She grabs my arm. "Hey, Laine. Chill, I'm only goofing around."

"It's not funny."

She looks so shocked as I scowl as her, and it's about time. It's about time I let her know she's being a fucking asshole.

"It's a fucking joke, alright?" She sighs, like I'm the unreasonable one. "I'm serious, I want to know. If it's a big deal for you, it's a big deal for me."

If only that were true. That's *never* been true.

I shrug, and why not. She's the best I've got.

"It was nice," I say. "He was really considerate, and really respectful, and took it really slow…"

"And…" Her hands are egging me on. "Juicy gossip, please…"

I lower my voice. "He kissed me…"

"Yes, and…"

"And it was amazing." I can't stop smiling. "*He* was amazing. He kissed me, and touched me, and…" I check there's nobody close. "And he put his mouth on me, and sucked my clit until I came, and then he put his dick there, and it was massive… really big…"

She laughs. "How would you know?"

I laugh right back. "I'm not a total baby, you know. I've watched *pornography*, just like you do."

"The very fact you call it pornography says it all."

"But he is," I continue. "He's big. And it felt amazing."

"But he didn't fuck you, with this big giant cock of his?" She raises an eyebrow.

I grin. "Not yet, but he will."

She groans. "So what *did* he do with it?"

The memories come back, and so do the tingles, the feeling of him, rubbing, and making those noises. The sound of the bed creaking.

"He rubbed me… right against my clit… and I came… and he came…"

"He fucking dry humped you?!"

I shrug. "It wasn't so dry…"

"Gross," she says, but she's lying. She's scowling again.

I sigh, hug my lunchbox to my chest. "I love him."

"Excuse me? You fucking what?!"

I smile. Simply. "I love him."

She stares at me like I'm a simpleton. Mum stares at me like that, too, and I hate it. I always hate it. "I mean it," I tell her. "I love him, and he loves me."

"You don't even *know* him," she snaps.

"I know enough," I snap back. "It's fate."

"Not those fucking horoscopes again…"

"I don't need horoscopes to tell me it's fate," I insist. "I already know. And he knows it, too."

"Then you're both fucking cray cray." She spins a finger in the air.

"He's going to be the one," I say, and I don't give a shit anymore. Not what she thinks, nor what she says. Not at how she looks at me, or how Mum looks at me, or how anyone else in the whole world looks at me.

None of it matters, not now I have Nick. *Daddy.*

Not now I have someone who loves me.

"Fine," Kelly Anne says finally, and lets out a sigh. "If you insist on being cray cray with Hannibal-old-guy then you do that. Just let me have all the juicy gossip, deal?"

I think I've won some invisible battle, and I'm not even sure what I was fighting.

"Sure," I say. "But his name's Nick."

"*Daddy Nick,*" she laughs, and I'm sure my burning cheeks are going to give me away, but she slaps me on the back and doesn't even notice. "Alright," she says. "Now, let's talk about blowjobs, I've got some great techniques…"

***

CHAPTER FOURTEEN

Laine

Nick's smiling when I slip into the passenger seat, and I can't stop giggling as Kelly Anne's silly-arse blowjob techniques flash back through my mind.

"What?" he asks. "What's got you so tickled?"

I shake my head, and try to stop, but he leans toward me, his eyes so questioning, and it's too much. It's much too much.

"Kelly Anne," I say, and he sighs before I've even started. "No!" I tell him, "it's funny. She was, um… trying to teach me… in the toilets…"

He raises an eyebrow. "Trying to teach you what exactly, Laine?"

The giggles stop as I realise I've committed myself to sharing the stupid story. And with that comes the truth that I've been blabbing about us, about what we did. It feels like I've done wrong somehow, like I shouldn't be talking about *that*, and I guess my expression says so, because his eyes won't leave mine.

"What, Laine?"

I shrug. "I, um… I told Kelly Anne, some things."

He nods. "Some things about us?"

I tap the empty lunchbox in my lap. "I won't tell her anything else… not if it's private…"

"Do you want us to be private?"

I shrug again. "If that's what you want…"

His hand rests on my arm. "That's not answering my question. Do *you* want us to be private?"

I don't. I don't want us to be private. I want to shout it from the rooftops, show the whole world that a man like Nick loves me, and I'm his and he's mine. But I don't say that. The words don't come, so I shake my head, hoping my eyes tell him all that.

"No," I say. "I don't want us to be private, like we're doing something wrong. I want it to be… real…"

He smiles. "It *is* real. *We're* real." His fingers squeeze my elbow. "I have no problem with you telling Kelly Anne about us, Laine, but you should be aware that aspects of our… *relationship*… may make people uncomfortable."

"I didn't tell her about… those bits…" I admit, and my cheeks are on fire.

"Probably for the best." He squeezes again. "I'm not ashamed, sweetheart, but we're unorthodox. Our relationship is unorthodox. Be prepared for what that means, should it get out somehow."

"It won't…" I tell him. "I'd only talk to Kelly Anne, and she'd…"

"She'd what?"

I don't want to say it, but I do. "She'd laugh, or be super icked out. She wouldn't get it."

He laughs, and it surprises me. "*Super icked out* could arguably

be the right response to a situation like ours. Daddy play is… *niche*, Laine, so niche that most people just wouldn't understand."

I laugh with him, but I'm shaking my head. "No! It's not super icky, not at all! I like it… it's just…"

"A little bit icky?"

"No!" I fidget in my seat. "I meant it's private, not icky."

Daddy play. The words spin in my brain, and they make sense. That's what this is. It's Daddy play. I saw that on Jerry Springer once, years ago, some grown up woman in pigtails, colouring in while this guy talked to Jerry about how she was his *little-y* or something.

It made me feel squirmy, all weird and hot, and then so guilty when Mum laughed about it and said how gross it was. Window cleaner guy, that's who she said it to. And he hadn't said a word, just stared in my direction.

"Let's go home," Nick says, and my thoughts are right back with him. He's looking at me so intently as he puts the car in gear, like he knows I'm feeling all squirmy again at the memory.

I nod. "Home sounds real good."

"Yes," he says. "It does."

And in that moment he's *that* Nick again. The Daddy Nick that rubbed his cock against me until he came.

***

Nick

She's thinking about it, the *Daddy play*. I can see it all over her face. I can feel it in her wispy little breaths, her eyes staring at me as I make

fast work of the drive home.

She's thinking about it and she likes it.

I imagine her horny little clit. Imagine her damp white knickers. Imagine the way she's clenching her thighs under the lunchbox in her lap.

"I'm going to shave you," I tell her.

"Okay," she says without hesitation, as though I've told her we're having chicken for dinner.

But I want more than that. My cock is craving a reaction, my cock is craving *her*. Craving the guilty devilment in her eyes when she knows she's my horny little girl.

"I'm going to shave your pretty little cunt, Laine, and then I'm going to suck on that smooth little mound until you come for your daddy like a good girl."

Her mouth drops open, her cheeks bloom red, and it makes me so fucking hard.

"That's what you want, isn't it? Tell Daddy that's what you want."

Her voice is so delicate. "Yes… yes, please…"

"I need more than that, Laine…Yes please, *Daddy*. I want you to shave me and lick me, *Daddy*. I'll be a good girl, *Daddy*."

She shifts in her seat and clears her throat, and her sweet excitement is too much for me. I take her lunchbox and throw it onto the backseat, and my fingers slip between her legs, rubbing at her through the denim of her jeans.

"*Yes please, Daddy*," she whispers, so softly, and her legs part, her hips rolling up for more.

"You like that, Laine? You like being my little girl?"

She nods, her lip pinched between her teeth. It takes all of my restraint to pull my hand away and turn my attention back to the road.

"I saw it… on the TV…" Her voice is hushed, confessional. "I saw it… this woman… in pigtails… and this guy… being her daddy…"

"Did it make you wet?"

She nods again. "I went to bed and touched myself, and it felt… icky… but nice…"

"*Dirty*," I tell her. "The word is *dirty*."

"Dirty…" she repeats. "It felt dirty… but nice… I couldn't stop."

"You don't have to stop. We can play that game forever, Laine. You can be my dirty little girl forever."

"Forever…" Dainty fingers reach out and stroke my hand on the gearstick.

"Daddy's going to make you his, Laine. Daddy's going to fuck you, and love you, and punish you when you're bad. Daddy will take care of you, sweetheart. I'll make it feel so nice when you're good, and make it hurt so bad when you're not. That's what you need, Laine. Love and discipline. That's what all little girls need from their daddy."

"Yes, Daddy…" Her breaths are like gasps. "Please… that's what I want… that's what I always wanted… I want *this*… I want it so bad…"

My cock is straining and my heartbeat is thumping in my temples. Everything is twitching, pounding, on the verge of exploding, all because of this divine little creature I picked up in the rain.

I should stop.

We should stop. Stop this perverted little game we're playing.

But stopping is the last thing I want.

***

141

Laine

He doesn't do any of the usual stuff, like head through to the kitchen. He doesn't head upstairs and take his jacket off and hang it up, or take my lunchbox and put it in the dishwasher. He doesn't make himself a coffee or get me a juice, or ask me about my day.

When Daddy Nick closes the front door today, he takes my hair in his hand and pulls tight until I gasp, and then he kisses me, and his tongue is so rough and so fast, his thigh between mine as he pins me to the wall in the hallway.

I wonder if this is it. If he'll really take me now.

If he'll take me here, with my jeans around my ankles and his tongue in my mouth. I want that. I want it any way he wants to give it to me.

His fingers tug at my cami top and squeeze my tits through my bra, and he's so hard against my belly, so hard and so big.

Suddenly Kelly Anne's silly techniques don't seem so silly.

I want to try them. Every single one of them.

I open my mouth wide for Daddy, let him push his tongue so deep, squirming against his leg as his fingers tug and pinch at my nipples. I like it. I like it so much when he's rough like this.

I wonder what it would feel like to be a bad girl and have him punish me, and I like that, too.

I groan as he pulls away, and his breath is hot in my face. Hot and fast.

"Upstairs," he orders. "Take your clothes off in the kitchen and wait for me at the table."

I nod and my tummy lurches as I leave him. He watches me all the way upstairs as the butterflies flutter. My heart thumps as I take off my cardigan on the way, and my cami, too. I fold them and place them on the chair, then unclip my bra with shaky fingers. I slip down my jeans and step out of them, my knickers, too, and put them on the pile until I'm only in my socks.

I'm tugging them off when he comes into view, and he stares at me. Swallows as I pull them free and put them on the chair with my knickers.

He's carrying a towel, and a bowl.

And a razor.

He's carrying a razor.

I feel so exposed as he comes near. His suit is so fine and his hair is so slick, and mine's a wispy mess. I brush it from my face as he watches. His eyes glint as he pats the table, and I hitch up and onto it, the wood so hard against my ass.

"Lie back, legs up," he tells me, and I do as he says, grabbing hold of my knees and holding them tight to my chest like I did last night.

He rolls me backwards, and slips a towel under my ass, and it feels so icky... *dirty*... like I'm a baby on a changing mat, and he's about to wipe my dirty bottom...

I wonder if he can see my... see *it*...

I wonder if he wants to...

He runs his fingers down my thighs, all the way to my pussy, and further. And I know then that he can. He can see everything.

He pulls my ass cheeks apart and it makes me screw my eyes closed, knowing he's looking at me there... knowing he can see the most private parts of me...

"Relax," he says. "No secrets from Daddy, remember? I want to see everything, know everything. Every beautiful dirty little part of you."

I feel heady. Nervous. My throat is dry and my feet are twitchy as he runs his thumb across my asshole. My actual asshole. And it tickles, but it's a nice tickle.

I don't know if it should feel this good, but it does… it feels really good.

"Dirty little girls like Daddy's cock in their ass, Laine."

He says it so bluntly, his voice so deep and strong. It makes my toes tingle, to think of him… in there…

"Good little girls are lucky because they get it nice and gentle."

The question rolls off my tongue. "And bad little girls..?"

I can hear the smile in his voice. "Be good and you won't have to find out."

His thumb, back and forth, pressing into my ass, and I like it. I like being a dirty girl.

I open my eyes, and his are fixed between my legs, right where he's touching. He looks so different like this, so dark and sexy and fierce, so different from the Daddy Nick that makes my lunchbox and strokes my hair at night.

"Wait right here," he says, like that's necessary.

He picks up the bowl and heads out of view, and I bounce my knees against my chest while I wait. I hear water running, and footsteps, my neck craning for sight of him. Steam rises from the bowl when he comes back into view, and there are those tingles in my toes again, those wings beating in my belly.

I peer down between my thighs as he lathers soap into his hands. They feel so warm as they touch against my pussy, so gentle as he rubs suds all over me. He meets my eyes as he takes the razor.

"Relax, sweetheart. I'll be careful."

I nod. "I know you will, Daddy."

It feels so strange, the sensation of the blade against my skin. Long

strokes, then short ones, his fingers spreading me open to run the razor between my lips. I trust him so much that it's easy to relax. I stare in fascination, not fear. Watching him, watching the way he's so careful and precise, watching the smile on his face as he shaves me bald and makes me so tender.

I flinch as the razor dips between my ass cheeks, and then I giggle for being so silly.

"Nice and smooth," he says, and runs the blade everywhere. *Everywhere.*

He wipes me down with a warm cloth and it feels like tingly heaven. Like my skin's never been touched before. I want to feel it for myself, but I don't move, just hold my knees tight like he asked me to.

"Beautiful," he says. "You're absolutely beautiful, little Laine."

He dips his head and blows warm breath on me, and it makes me shudder and squirm.

"Tingles…" I whisper. "It all tingles…"

He lets out a groan as he presses his lips to my pussy, and it's so raw that it makes my head spin. His tongue swirls and laps at me, his fingers spreading me open until he's flicking my clit with fast little strokes and I'm gripping my knees so tight my fingers hurt.

"Yes, Daddy… please…"

His mouth is hot as he clamps it onto me, and he sucks hard. I make stupid hissing noises as he pinches my clit between his teeth, and my muscles are clenched tight, my hips bucking, desperate for more.

It's easy to come today. My body just does it, my breath fast and short, my legs trembling as I go up and over the edge. *He* makes it so easy.

I jump as his tongue touches my asshole, squirming away before he realises he's made a mistake and squicks out, but he grabs my thighs and holds me tight, and his tongue is right back there, tasting me, in my dirtiest place, where it feels so icky… *dirty…*

"Daddy…" I whisper, as though I need to tell him, but he just grunts and pushes the point of his tongue right there, right inside.

His voice is muffled and gruff. "Relax," he says. "Let Daddy taste you."

And he can't mean… but he does… he does mean it. His fingers spread my ass and his tongue pushes and pokes its way inside, and it feels like an electric eel, all sparky and tickly and jolty.

And I can't get enough.

I can't get enough of how it feels.

He knows it, too. I hear a low laugh. "Daddy knows how to make you feel good, sweetheart."

He pushes in deeper and I can't stop myself moaning.

I gasp as he pulls away. He licks his lips as I stare at him, and I wonder what I taste like.

But I don't think I want to know.

I drop my knees and let my legs hang over the edge of the table. I'm propped up on my elbows as Daddy Nick unbuckles his belt.

"Do you want to make Daddy feel good?"

I smile so brightly, because it's real and true. There's nothing I want more than to make Daddy feel good.

He beckons me off the table, and his hand lands on my head, pushes me down to my knees, and I know what's coming. I just hope I remember what Kelly Anne told me.

His cock is so big when he pulls it free. He smells all grown up, and his cock is dark and thick and veiny. He works it in his hand and the end is wet, just a little. The slit in the end is so close to my face, and I wonder if I could fit the tip of my tongue in there, and if I'd want to.

Yes, I'd want to.

My mouth opens on instinct, my eyes moving up to meet his as his

fingers stroke my hair.

"Give me your mouth, little Laine," he says, and his hips push forward, the big, dark head of his cock aiming right for my lips. "Look at Daddy now. Keep looking at Daddy."

He's bigger in my mouth than I expect, pushing past my teeth until my cheeks billow and strain, and I want to retch but fight it, just try to keep breathing through my nose as he rocks himself back and forth.

"That's it, sweetheart. That's a good girl."

He pushes to the back of my throat and I splutter until he pulls out again.

"Suck Daddy. Suck Daddy with that pretty little mouth."

I do suck him. I suck him hard, not caring how my mouth is wet and slurpy. Not caring that my eyes are watering and my cheeks feel hollow with the strain.

I forget every single piece of advice Kelly Anne gave me, because it's all I can do to keep sucking as he takes my hair and holds me tight. He thrusts, slowly, but deep, gently, back and forth.

"That's it… good girl…" He closes his eyes and lets out a grunt. "Deeper, let Daddy deeper."

I retch as he pushes, but don't pull away. I never want to pull away.

He pushes his dick into my cheek until it strains, and then he watches me. Watches me with his big thick cock stretching my mouth, and I pray I'm doing it right, pray I'm good enough.

"Perfect," he growls. "Fuck, Laine, you're a fucking treasure."

His pleasure is the greatest sound on earth. The roughness of his fingers in my hair is the greatest feeling. I love it when he grunts and groans, when he thrusts and makes me gag.

I love it when he loses control and his hips jerk and thrust and his dick twitches and pulses in my mouth.

I love the filthy noises it makes when he's fucking my mouth.

Because that's what he's doing. He's fucking my mouth.

My fingers can't stop playing with my clit, and my bare pussy feels so strange and sensitive. I'm making noises too, weird little gasps that sound like squeaks as his balls slap off my chin.

They're bigger than I thought, too.

"Daddy's going to come," he rasps. "You want Daddy's cum, don't you?"

I can barely nod, but I try anyway.

"It's coming… take it all for Daddy, take it all, sweetheart…"

It hits the back of my tongue first, and it's thick and salty and makes me choke. I feel him spurt against my lips, and it tastes so strange, like nothing I've ever tasted.

"Open for Daddy…" he groans, and there's more. I open wide as his dick jerks and his cum fills my mouth, and it's warm under my tongue, my eyes streaming as it trickles to the back of my throat.

He grunts and swears and works his cock as it spurts, over and over, and then he tenses and sighs. He smooths the hair from my forehead and smiles at me.

"Show me, show Daddy."

I open my mouth wide, and he looks inside, then pushes his fingers in, rolls them around my tongue where I'm full of him.

"Good girl…" he says, and it makes my heart so proud. "Swallow for Daddy."

I swallow it all down like a good little girl and show him my empty mouth, and it's really not that bad. It's not so bad at all, not like Kelly Anne said it was.

I like Daddy Nick's cum, just as much as I like the rest of him.

He pulls me to my feet and wraps me in his arms, and I feel so giddy, so floaty and light as he holds me tight.

He kisses my mouth, where he's been, and I'm sure I must taste of him, but he doesn't care. His tongue licks at mine, and mine licks his right back, and I'm giggling, happy.

I'm still giggling as he pulls away.

"You can do your homework before dinner," he says, and dirty Daddy Nick is all gone.

***

CHAPTER FIFTEEN

Nick

I watch her as I cook up our pasta, chopping tomatoes as she pretends to ponder over an assignment. She's not thinking about her college work, not even close. Her eyes flick in my direction every time she thinks I'm occupied, and her cheeks are still pretty pink, flushed with that beautiful post-orgasmic glow every man likes to see after he's been eating pussy.

She's barely dressed, and I wonder if her camisole, knickers and socks combination is deliberate. She couldn't look more *innocent little girl* if she tried. It shouldn't feel as good as it does, this *thing* we've got. It shouldn't feel as though my life meant nothing before she was here, but it does.

"What is it?" she asks, and she's smiling.

"Sorry?"

She laughs, and it's intoxicating. "You're staring so hard it burns. Have I done something?"

"You've done plenty, young lady," I tell her in my sternest voice.

"I have?"

"Oh yes." I continue chopping, then put the tomatoes in the pan before I smile. "All of it good."

She sighs and feigns a heart attack. "I'm glad it's all good," she says. "You've done plenty too, *Daddy Nick*."

"I have, have I?"

She nods, and there's no laughter there, just a hushed little whisper. "I was nobody before you found me."

It hits me in the gut. Two different people, two very different worlds. Both empty.

She taps the pen I gave her against her notepad. "I never had a family before, but now I have. We're a family, right, a little one, me and you?"

"Yes, Laine. Yes we are."

Her smile is bright enough to light the world. I know I'll never grow tired of looking at her, never tire of taking care of her, or holding her tight. Or loving her.

"Thanks," she says. "You've given me everything."

"And I'll take *you*." I tell her. "Soon."

"Soon?"

I nod. "Soon, Laine."

"But not today?"

"Not today."

She shrugs. "Ok, Daddy. Whenever you're ready."

Her coy little grin makes me smile all the while I strain the pasta.

***

I run her a bath full of bubbles, and she's so dainty as she dips a toe in.

"Too hot?"

She shakes her head. "Just right."

She holds my arm for balance, even though she doesn't need it, and I hold her as she lowers herself, her tight little body making my cock strain as she disappears under the suds.

I uncuff my shirt as she watches, roll up my sleeves before I dip the jug in the water between her legs. She sits up instinctively, tipping her head back ready for me to wet her hair.

"Mum used to do this," she tells me. "Only sometimes, when I was little. We didn't have a shower." She closes her eyes as I tip the jug. "That feels really nice."

"Our new routine, sweetheart," I say. "Bath and bedtime." The thought thrills me.

I squeeze the shampoo onto her hair, darker now it's wet, and it feels so soft against my fingers as I lather.

"That feels better than nice," she tells me. "It feels amazing."

I massage her scalp, and tickle her neck, twist her golden tresses around my fingers as she sighs.

She lowers herself under the water to rinse it off, and her knees bob up. I resist the urge to slip my hand between her legs, and she surfaces none the wiser of the hard on pulsing in my trousers. I smooth through the conditioner as she sighs.

"Did you do this… for Jane?"

"Yes, I did."

"That's nice," she says.

"Like riding a bike," I tell her, making sure I've conditioned the fine little wisps at her temples. "Once you know how to wash hair, you never forget."

"You're good at it. You're good at everything."

"Not everything."

She twists her head to meet my eyes. "Yes so. You're amazing."

She can say it all she likes, but the two people I loved so much are still in the ground because I didn't take good enough care of them. She must notice the sadness, because she twists further, and her sweet little nipples greet me through the bubbles.

"I really mean it. You're amazing, Daddy. So kind and thoughtful and strong."

"Not strong enough, Laine. Not in the past. Not enough to enforce the discipline I should've enforced."

Her eyes are wide, lashes wet. "But you are now."

"Yes," I tell her. "I am now."

She twists back as I continue with her hair. "How will you… discipline me…"

I don't hesitate. "I'll spank you, Laine. Hard. Until you learn whatever lesson needs learning."

The water gives her away, a slop against the sides as she squeezes her legs together. "You'll spank me?"

"Hard." I tug her hair back until her eyes are staring up at mine. "My father used a belt on me. It's in my study, which still has the same desk he used to punish me over."

She swallows. "It must've hurt."

"Very much." I let go of her hair. "But he taught me well. Taught me

how to be smart, and dedicated, and driven."

"Will you… use a belt on me?"

"If you deserve it." I twist her hair into a pony then pile it on top of her head and grab the soap. "Be a good girl and there'll be no need. Arms up."

She raises her arms and I soap her, from her dainty fingers to her elbows, then up to her armpits as she giggles. "That tickles."

She stops giggling as my fingers work down her front. I take her sweet little tits and roll them in my palms, and her nipples are hard, just right for a little pinch. She leans into me and I pinch them again, sharp enough that she squeaks.

"Dirty girl," I tell her, and tap her knees. "Let Daddy wash you."

She raises herself on her arms, her back arched and knees spread without hesitation. Her pussy presents itself above the water, covered in bubbles and rosy pink from the warmth. I lather fresh soap and slip my hand between her thighs, rubbing back and forth, where my fingers catch her clit and slide between her puffy lips. She rocks, and murmurs, eyes tight shut as I soap her.

"Lovely and clean," I tell her, but she keeps rocking.

"Please, Daddy… that feels so nice…"

"Does my dirty little girl want Daddy to make her come?"

She nods her head. "Please, Daddy…"

I pull my hand away and she groans. "On all fours, be a good girl and I'll make you come."

The water sloshes as she twists and rolls over. She raises herself so beautifully, and I change position, stepping to the other end of the bath where her ass is waiting for me. I pick up the moisturiser from the shelf, and squirt some onto my fingers. She spreads her knees as far as they'll go, and the cheeks of her ass part for me. Her pussy lips drip underneath her, so beautifully puffy. I rub the moisturiser over the

tight globes of her ass, and she doesn't flinch as I part them to find her puckered little asshole. It winks at me, and I know she's nervous.

"Relax," I tell her. "Let Daddy wash you."

She nods, lets out a gasp as I run my fingers across her tight little ring. "Relax," I repeat, and she tries, her muscles loosening as I rub the cream along her crack. She shifts forward when I squirt a dollop right on target. "Be good," I warn, and she hitches back.

"What are you going to do?" she asks, and her voice is crackly. Glorious nerves.

"Let Daddy in, sweetheart." I press my finger to that gorgeous virgin ass, and it's clenched tight. So fucking tight.

"But I'm… it's dirty… what if it's…"

I lower my voice. "Laine, be a good girl, let Daddy in."

A moment I'll savour forever. My beautiful girl rocking on her knees as her breath catches in her throat. Hesitant. Divine.

Horny.

Her pussy clenches. Her asshole winks.

And then relaxes.

"I'll be a good girl, Daddy," she says.

***

Laine

He's going to put his fingers in there, and I want it. It feels so dirty but I want it.

Daddy Nick wants to put his fingers in my asshole, just like he put

156

his tongue in there. But his fingers are big.

Not as big as his cock.

I breathe, and make myself relax, and he groans.

He's horny Daddy Nick again, and if my weight wasn't on my arms I'd put my fingers back there and touch myself. My clit is tickling, little sparks that make my breath come out raspy.

I feel his finger pressing against my hole, and it feels so hot. He pushes and I make a funny little grunt as I feel it slide in a little way.

"Good girl," he says, and it makes me feel so warm.

He pushes again, and it feels so weird, squelchy from soap as he wriggles his finger then slides it further, and I feel him, going deeper. It feels like I need the toilet.

I tell him so and he lets out another one of those groans, and I need him to touch my pussy so bad that I can't stop myself moving.

"Oh yes," he whispers. "That's it. Push back for Daddy."

I ease my hips back and it feels hot, like a poker as it goes deeper. I groan and squeeze my eyes shut, and I really do need the toilet.

"Daddy… mmm… I… I need to…"

"No," he says. "You don't."

I gasp as he pushes again, and it hurts, just a bit. He keeps pushing, and I grit my teeth, and then he's all the way in, I know he is. It doesn't hurt anymore. He wriggles inside me, and I'm squelching. He presses and wriggles some more and I feel it in my pussy. It aches a fluttery ache.

And I like it.

I really like it.

"Beautiful," he whispers, and I feel so shy. "How does that feel?"

I don't know what to say.

"How does it feel, Laine? Tell Daddy."

He wriggles some more and I am so scared I'm going to poop on his finger that I clench real tight, and that makes the ache in my pussy so much worse.

I moan, and I don't sound like me at all.

"Tell Daddy, Laine."

"I… I like it…"

"Tell Daddy how it feels to have his finger in your ass, sweetheart."

Squirmy. It's so hot and squirmy… and amazing…

"It feels…" I suck in breath as he slides it in and out. "Ah… Ah, Daddy… that feels so nice…"

In and out, in and out, and it doesn't hurt, not even a bit, not even uncomfortable like it did at first…

"That's right, sweetheart, take it. Take it for Daddy."

I move as he moves, the water splashing under me as I jerk against Daddy's thick finger as he squirms it inside me, and then there's his thumb, pressing against my pussy, right against my clit, and I can't stand it, I can't stop grunting.

"Daddy's going to make you come. You're such a good girl, Laine, such a good little girl."

I feel on fire, my ass clenching and my pussy too, and my breath in rasps. "*Daddy… Daddy, please… don't stop… don't stop, Daddy…*"

I don't recognise myself, and I can't stop, can't stop begging as he rubs me and pushes his finger in and out.

And then there's more… I feel another finger, and I groan but don't stop moving… and it hurts, a burn as he pushes that one in too.

"Daddy's going to fuck your ass, Laine," he grunts. I wonder if he means right now and I don't care. He could put anything in there and I wouldn't care. "Soon, sweetheart, soon Daddy's going to give you his

cock."

"*Please...*" I hiss. "Oh God, Daddy, please don't stop! Please don't stop!"

I slam forward as he makes me come, slopping water over the side, and my hair is slimy with conditioner, pressed to my cheek as Daddy fucks me with his fingers and my ass burns and tightens. I'm a shuddery mess, my mouth open as he keeps circling my clit, and I want him in me. I want him in my pussy.

I want Daddy's cock inside me.

"*Yes...*" I whisper. "*Oh, Daddy, yes...*"

I jerk, and wriggle and hiss. His fingers keep on fucking my ass. My clit tickles and pulses and I cry out, my legs trembling.

And then I'm done.

I breathe.

He pulls his fingers out with a squelch, and my ass feels open wide. I can feel where he's been.

He gives my ass a slap. "Time to wash that conditioner out," he says.

I roll over and tip my head back like a good girl.

***

CHAPTER SIXTEEN

Laine

He towels me dry and helps me into my knickers and nightdress. My socks, too. He gets me a glass of warm milk and takes me through to the sitting room, pats his knee as he lowers himself into an armchair, and I join him, my ass pressing into his lap as his arms wrap me up and hold me tight.

His lips press to my shoulder. "You smell so clean, Laine. Sweet, like cherries."

He breathes in my damp hair and I still can't believe this is real. I can't believe that someone really loves me like this.

He takes a brush from the side table and its bristles feel so nice against my scalp as he works it through my hair. He's gentle, but firm, long smooth strokes to my shoulder blades, pulling loose any knots with short, sharp tugs. He's done this before.

I'm surprised when he splits my hair into three, his fingers so quick at plaiting the length. I hear the twang of a hairband from his wrist

161

and he ties the end.

"Wavy curls in the morning," he tells me. "Like an angel."

"Thanks, Daddy Nick."

Daddy Nick.

Nick.

Using his name that way is my one pathetic safeguard of being… I dunno… being his lover, not just his little girl. I want to cling onto that, and I guess it's fear. Fear of him seeing me as just a baby. That's what I feel like, his baby girl.

And I love that.

I really love that.

But I want to be his lover, too.

His *actual* lover.

"You're tense," he comments. "What's up, sweetheart?"

"Nothing," I say.

He sighs. "No secrets, Laine."

I shrug. "I guess I'm just scared."

"Of what?"

"Of loving being your little girl so much that it becomes everything I am." My own honesty surprises me.

"Would that be so bad?"

I shrug again. I picture the kind of women he works with. Important, smart women. Successful women. *Grown up* women.

"This is for keeps," he whispers. "You and me." His chin rests on my shoulder, his breath warm against my cheek. "Now that I've found you, Laine, I'm not ever letting you go."

"And that's what you want? A little girl… to take care of…"

"I want *you*," he says.

I twist until I can face him, and his eyes are so warm and kind. "I feel like I could stay like this forever. Never grow up. But how could that work?"

He trails a finger down my cheek. "You're thinking too much, sweetheart. Worrying unnecessarily."

Butterflies again, so many butterflies. "I guess I've never had to worry about losing anything before. Never had anything worth keeping."

"You won't lose this, Laine. Finding you made life mean something again."

I smile. "It did? Really?"

"Really." His eyes smile back at me. "Now, stop your worrying and drink your milk. It's bedtime."

I bury my face into his neck where it feels so nice, and he holds me tight and kisses my hair while I breathe him in, and my butterflies calm their flapping.

"Thanks, Daddy."

***

I wake up from a horrible nightmare. A horrible nightmare where Nick's introducing me to my new *mummy*. And she's beautiful, and stylish and smart and all grown up.

She's wearing heels and red lipstick, and carries a briefcase, and her smile is pearly white as she holds out a hand to me.

He's still sleeping soundly when I open my eyes, his breathing calm and steady, his chest to my back. I don't want to wake him, so I don't. Just snuggle into his arms and tell myself I'm being stupid, that being a

little-y doesn't mean I'm not a proper lover. We can talk, about things. Grown up things.

I could learn to be like Kelly Anne, and put on some lipstick and some sexy underwear and show him I'm a woman.

If I wanted to.

And that's the thing. I'm not sure I want to.

I love the way it feels to be his little girl. I love how naughty it feels, and how safe I feel.

I love how it makes him grunt, and makes his eyes so dark, and his cock so big and hard.

I love Daddy Nick.

And that's what I'm really scared of. Of loving someone as much as this so quickly. Because if I can love him this much already, when I don't even know him, not really, how much am I going to love him when I'm used to him being my everything?

He shifts in his sleep, and his arms tighten around my waist.

He's already my everything. All other things feel so far away. My old house, my old babysitting routine, Kelly Anne and her chitchat. My mum…

I haven't even given her my new number, and she hasn't tried to reach me. No ping on social media, or desperate message through Kelly Anne. Nothing.

I exist only to Nick.

And that's where I want to stay. Forever. Right here.

In his little girl's bedroom, with its pink walls and its comfy bed and its pretty things.

Sugar and spice and all things nice.

That's what *I'll* be made of.

And Daddy Nick will love me for it. Forever.

Just like he would've loved his own little girl.

***

Nick

Our routine is blissful, Laine's and mine. Pulling free from her arms in the morning to shower and cook her up some breakfast. Dropping her at college and kissing her hair and telling her to have a nice day. Her sweet voice at lunchtime, our telephone call like clockwork, one on the dot. Her joyful recounting of her day when I pick her up. The quiet beauty of her completing her assignments at the dinner table.

Our evening meal. Our gentle conversations.

The chores she's taken up naturally. Loading the dishwasher after our meal. Setting the table for the next. Dropping her clothes in the laundry hamper. Fastening up my cufflinks with a smile.

Laine is everything I could have wished for. She's straight from my dreams.

And she's mine.

All mine.

My innocent, perfect little girl.

But there's a dirtiness behind her sexual naivety. A naughty little girl behind her angel eyes.

It's in the way she wriggles and squirms and moans for my tongue, for my kisses, for my dirty fingers in her ass. She begs like she's wanton and starved, and it's a balm to my filthy soul, taking all of my restraint not to spear her tight little virgin pussy whenever she's spread underneath me. She takes everything *Daddy* gives her, and still her ass

grinds against my cock in the night, wanting more. Always wanting more.

And tonight's the night she's going to get it.

Friday night was always my plan. An unexpected surprise for my sweetheart after a long week at college.

She's none the wiser as I collect her from the college gates, telling me all about her day as she piles into the passenger seat. Kelly Anne this, and Kelly Anne that. Always that cow Kelly Anne.

I say nothing tonight, just smile softly until she realises I'm quieter than usual.

"What is it, Daddy?" Her eyes are so adoringly worried.

"I'm taking you out," I tell her. "Anywhere you want to go. My treat."

Her grin is magical. "Our for dinner?"

I nod. "Anywhere you want to go."

I can feel her stewing, contemplating her options, and I know her well enough by now to know she's wondering what *I* want to do, where *I'd* like to eat.

"Where *you* want to go, Laine," I tell her. "We'll go where *I* want to go a different night."

"Okay," she says, and I feel her eyes on me. I know the smile on her lips, the hint of devilment. "Milkshake and a burger. Fries, too."

I knew it. I laugh as I tell her as much.

"A drive through!" she expands. "Oh please, Daddy Nick, can we go to a drive through?"

"And eat greasy fries in our lovely clean car?"

She nods. "Please, please, please!"

"If that's what you want."

She grins, bounces in her seat. "It is! It's exactly what I want!"

"Then a drive through it is," I tell her.

I make her do her homework before we head out to eat, and there's a thrill of excitement in her smile which makes me both so happy and sad in parallel. Such a simple pleasure, and yet it means so much to my sweet Laine.

She skips out to the car when I tell her it's time to go. Her cheeks are flushed and her smile is bright.

"I'm so looking forward to this," she tells me as she buckles herself in.

"So, what's on the Laine Seabourne menu for this evening? Burger, fries, milkshake? How about some of those chicken nuggets on the side?"

She nods. "And an apple pie, too? Please can we have an apple pie?"

"We can have whatever you want, sweetheart. Ten apple pies if you like."

She lets out a squeal. "A large milkshake! Maybe even two!"

"And large fries, *extra large* fries. *Double* fries. Fries on fries."

She laughs. "And what will you have?"

I shrug. "I don't usually eat fast food, I'll take your guidance."

"Don't worry, Daddy Nick," she giggles. "I'll help you out."

She does help me out, leaning across me to reach the drive through intercom and dishing out the order. Her hand rests on my thigh and my cock strains as she lets them know we want extra everything, and she doesn't want gherkin on her burger and neither do I.

She claps her hands as I ease the car towards the collection point.

"Thank you," she says. "You have no idea how much I love this stuff."

"I'm getting the picture. We can do this every weekend, if you love it so much."

Her eyes widen. "Every weekend? Seriously?"

"Seriously. If you're a good girl."

She lurches from her seat and wraps her arms around my neck, as though I've just proposed marriage. My stomach lurches and my dick twitches and there's a glorious pang in my heart.

"Thank you, Daddy Nick."

I squeeze her knee as we reach the collection window. "It's just a bit of fast food, Laine. I have so many amazing pleasures to show you, I promise. We'll do it all, sweetheart. Everything. Fast food will be the last thing on your to-do list."

I pass her the tray of food and thank and pay the attendant, and then I park up in the carpark as Laine instructs, and I genuinely have no idea why we didn't just eat in. I tell her so.

"It's different in the car," she tells me.

"How so?"

She shrugs, her fingers busy sorting out our order. "Because a drive through is... cooler..."

"Cooler?"

"Yeah, more... I dunno..."

I laugh as a couple of fries spill between her knees and land in the footwell. "More messy?"

She giggles. "Well, yeah. That too. But it's magical, getting your order and eating it on your lap in the car."

I'm not sure I see the magic in getting grease all over your dashboard, but I smile regardless. "Did you do this with your mum?"

She shakes her head. "With a couple of her boyfriends, when it was all new. You know how it goes. New guy, wants to impress the kid, takes the family out for burgers, reads a bedtime story. Gets bored after a week and sends the kid to bed early every night until they get bored of the mum too and vanish into the horizon forever."

I don't know how it goes. I don't know at all. "That's rough, Laine."

"It's alright," she says. "I did ok. I had it pretty good, loads of other kids have it way worse."

I keep quiet, unwrapping the thing that could only loosely be described as a burger and contemplating how she can possibly find so much pleasure in this.

She gives a delightful groan as she bites into hers, a look of bliss on her face that I hope I'll remember forever.

"Good?" I ask.

More groans. She nods her head, chews then swallows. "Better than good. Amazing."

I bite into mine. It's actually not that bad, if you like the taste of processed plastic. Her eyes question me, and I haven't the heart to tell her so. "Good," I say, and she laughs. It's raw and real and beautiful.

"Liar!"

I hold up my hands. "Really, it's good," I lie again.

Her eyes sparkle. She hands me my milkshake. "Try this. You'll like this."

It's thick and slurpy. More sugar than substance.

"So?" she prompts. "It's good, right?"

I tip my head. "It's better than the burger."

"I love milkshake. It's the best."

I can't resist, not when I see her hollow cheeks as she sucks in rapture, her eyelashes fluttering as she takes a greedy mouthful.

169

"I'm glad you think so," I tell her. "Because Daddy's got a milkshake of his own to give you later."

I try to keep my face impassive, try to stay stern, and serious, but her wide eyes tickle me. I laugh. Properly laugh, right from the belly.

"Gross," she says, but she's laughing, too, and it feels so good to let it all out, to see humour in a world that used to be so grey.

I feel alive again.

It dries up slowly, a soft giggle as she turns her attention back to her meal, and I'm staring at her, all thought of food long gone.

"Tonight," I tell her, and it takes her a moment to register my intention.

"Tonight? Really?!"

I nod. "Really. Home just as soon as we've finished."

She pauses, a fry halfway to her mouth, then drops it back in the carton and bundles the food back in the paper bag as I watch.

"Finish your dinner," I say. "There's no rush, sweetheart."

But she doesn't stop. Not until it's all away.

She takes my hand. Squeezes my greasy fingers with hers. "Please let's go home, Daddy. I'm not hungry anymore."

***

CHAPTER SEVENTEEN

Nick

She's nervous. I can feel it, her fingers squeezing mine so tightly as I lead her upstairs. I'd planned to take her in my room, in my big bed like a big girl, but the temptation to take her innocence in pretty pink sheets is too much to bear. She takes a breath as she steps through the doorway, and her smile is so bright, trying too hard to be confident. Her raspy breath gives her away.

I close the door behind us and my beautiful girl faces me as I flick on the lamp. Her hands are clasped in front of her, so unsure.

I shrug off my jacket and hang it on the back of the door. I loosen my tie slowly, and unbutton my shirt as she stares at me with wide eyes.

"Undress for Daddy," I tell her, and her nervous fingers are a joy to watch. They dither as they pull her top over her head, fumble as they pop the button on her jeans and ease down the zipper. She wriggles out of them and stands before me in just her underwear. Her bra is so understated, only the tiniest frill of lace on plain white. Her nipples

171

poke through the fabric, tiny little peaks that make my mouth water.

"Turn for Daddy, let me see you."

She smiles so shyly as she does a twirl, her shoulders back and proud, even though I'm sure her heart is racing in her chest. Her ass is a delight, tight young virgin cheeks just begging to be spanked. A dirty part of me wishes my sweet Laine was a naughty girl, but there'll be opportunity for punishment in good time. Even the most adorable little girls can't always be angels.

I'm beginning to read her expressions. The tiny twitch in the corner of her smile, the flutter of her eyelashes, the stare she gives when she's so eager for praise.

"Beautiful," I tell her as she finishes her twirl.

She breathes out a sigh of relief. "Thanks, Daddy Nick."

"It's just Daddy tonight," I tell her, and she nods.

"Okay, Daddy."

I undo my cufflinks and shrug off my shirt. Her mouth is open as I take off my belt, her weight shifting from foot to foot as I lower my trousers.

My cock is so ready for her, balls so fucking tight at the thought of taking her sweet little virgin pussy. I feel like a starving man, mouth watering over a tasty piece of rare steak. Tender, perfect, innocent.

The beast inside wants to take her rough and fast, to show her who she belongs to and instil some discipline right from the start. But I'm a better man than that.

Her arms are waiting as I step into them, her sweet fingers twisting in my hair as I kiss her pretty mouth. She murmurs as I give her my tongue, hers dancing such a delicate dance, then she moans as my fingers trail up her belly to squeeze at those little button nipples.

My horny girl is wet for me. She grinds against my bare thigh and the cotton of her knickers is soaking through. She humps me so

sweetly, a squirmy little package of need, but I ease her away, pressing my finger to her lips as she protests.

"All in good time, sweetheart. Easy now. Relax for Daddy."

I walk her to the bed, and she falls back without instruction. Her greedy little fingers rub at her clit through her sodden knickers. The fabric highlights her little pink slit so fucking beautifully.

"Dirty girl," I grunt, and work my cock slowly, from balls to tip. She's staring at the length of me, and those nerves are so plain to see. "Are you ready for Daddy, Laine?"

She nods. "I'm ready, Daddy. Really ready."

Her fingers keep playing as I kneel onto the bed alongside her, circling her clit so eagerly until I push them aside with my own. I press them into her slit, stretching that cotton fabric between her pussy lips as she squeezes her eyes shut.

I know I should take it slowly. I know I should take her with my fingers, one by one, until her pussy is open and willing. I know that's what a good daddy should do for his little girl, but right now I don't feel like such a good daddy.

I want my cock to be the first thing she feels. I want my cock to be the thing that breaks her. I want her to feel how big and hard Daddy's cock is for his gorgeous little girl.

"What is it, Daddy?" Her sweet smile makes my cock twitch.

"It's nothing, sweetheart," I tell her, resigning myself to be the better man.

But she won't let it go. She hitches herself up on her elbows, her eyes so wide.

"Am I doing something wrong? I'm not sure what to do…"

She looks scared. There's a shake in her voice.

"Taking my time, Laine. That's all. Just relax for me." I stroke her soft thigh and slip my hand inside her knickers. She moans and relaxes

to the bed.

"Daddy wants his cock to be the first thing you feel inside you, Laine. Daddy wants to feel your tight little pussy stretch for him for the very first time."

Her hand presses onto mine, right between her legs, urging my fingers to her horny little clit.

"I want that too…" It's barely more than a murmur, and it's not enough.

"It'll hurt," I tell her. "Daddy's cock is going to hurt unless I make your sweet little pussy ready for it."

"But I…" she whispers. "I don't care… I want what you want…"

I smile. "No, sweetheart. We'll do this right, for you."

She shakes her head, keeps coaxing my fingers between her legs. "You've given me so much, Daddy. I want to give you this… *me*… however you want it… I want it to be good for you, Daddy…"

I don't say a word, just keep circling that tight little bud until she shudders, so close to coming, so beautifully close.

"Please, Daddy… please…" Her request is so beautiful in her innocence, her desire to please me the most magical treasure. "I want it, Daddy, I promise…"

"Let me make you come," I tell her. "Let's make you nice and wet for Daddy's cock."

She's already sopping. Delicious squelches from her pussy make my cock so hard. I lower myself, until my mouth hovers over her soft little mound. I pull her knickers down her clammy thighs and she wriggles to help. The scent of her is divine. I breathe her in, my nose pressed into those soft lips, nudging at her clit until she gasps.

I spread her with my fingers, and suck that tight little nub into my mouth, suck hard and steady until her hips are thrusting and her fingers are tugging at my hair.

I wrap my arms under her thighs and hold her tight to my mouth, my tongue lapping at her slit as she moans. I suck again, and it's enough to make her cry out, and then she tumbles, jerking under me as she comes, her heels kicking at the bedcovers, back arched as she rides the waves.

"Oh, Daddy... yes... yes..."

She's so fucking beautiful like that. Her pussy clenches as I lick the wetness from her swollen clit, and I pepper her thighs with gentle kisses, right the way down to her toes.

Her eyes are hooded and adoring. She lays so still for me, so calm in her vulnerability.

Trust. It's a beautiful thing.

I take her ankles and position them at my hips. I spread her thighs, and she moans as I tease open her pussy lips, splaying her nice and wide. I soak in the sight of her untouched little hole for the last time, the delicate pink of her hymen the most precious gift I'll ever take.

I should say it, so I do. "We should use protection," I tell her. "I don't want to put you in a situation, Laine."

She doesn't flinch. "You mean a baby? You don't want to risk a baby?"

I laugh gently. "It's not about what I want, Laine. It's about you. What's right for you."

Her quizzical expression gives me the strangest rush. "But would you? I mean, not right now. I mean, in theory..."

This really isn't the time, not with my swollen cock bursting to take her virginity. "I'll give you whatever you want, Laine, but it's always going to be your decision."

"You'd give me a baby? If that's what I wanted?" She looks so surprised. I'm surprised she's so surprised.

"If that's what you wanted, sweetheart." I smile. "But I can use

something, for tonight, to be safe."

She grips my wrist as I begin to move away, and I stop. Wait.

"Please don't," she whispers. "Please don't use anything. I want it to be you inside me. Just you."

"If you're sure."

She nods. "I'm really sure."

My heart feels fit to burst. My balls straining, cock aching to be buried inside my sweet love. I squeeze her cute little tits, and the thought is there unbidden. The thought of those little breasts swollen with milk, her belly stretched with our baby. A baby inside my gorgeous little girl.

She takes a breath. "I want you so much, Daddy."

"And I want you, Laine. So very much, sweetheart."

I lift her knees to her chest for the perfect view of her gorgeous cunt. She's shaking, and she smiles as I realise.

"I'm not scared," she tells me. "It's just stupid nerves."

"A little bit of pain, sweetheart, that's all. It'll feel good after that, I promise."

I press the tip of my dick to her slit, rub it back and forth, teasing it inside just a little. I love the way she's so pink and puffy, the way her lips splay around my cock. I ease forward, and it's tight. So fucking tight.

She moans and grips at the bedsheets.

I'm hardly in and she feels so fucking divine. It takes every scrap of restraint not to shunt my length all the way. Slowly, an agonising tension as I position myself for greater leverage. Her pussy opens, she squeaks as my swollen head sinks inside.

"Ow, Daddy, that's big… it's really big…"

I move my hips, tiny nudges. "Let me in, sweetheart. Let Daddy

love you."

She takes a breath and I push harder. Hard enough to gain an inch. I nearly shoot my fucking load, she's so fucking tight.

She whimpers. She's tense, her whole body tense.

"Just relax and let Daddy in, Laine. Be a good girl for Daddy."

I stay still, wait, but when her eyes meet mine they are full of determination.

"Do it, Daddy," she hisses. "Do it!"

Her tone thrills me, my balls tighten. "Tell Daddy what you want, Laine. Tell me."

Her gaze is questioning, curious.

"Tell me, Laine. Be a dirty little girl for Daddy."

She tips her head back, and smiles through the nerves.

The girl knows exactly what I want.

"Fuck me, Daddy… please fuck me…"

A thrust. One hard fucking thrust and she squeals as her pussy takes me in. I watch myself sink into her, savour the magical moment I make her mine. That magical moment her hymen breaks and she squeals again and shudders and swears under her breath.

"Ow…" she mewls. "Ah… ah… *ow*… ow, it hurts!"

But it's done. I'm in, my cock buried deep in that tight little snatch. I ease down onto her, her sweet tits mashed to my chest, and her legs wrap me up, her arms too.

"Good girl," I whisper. "You're such a good girl. Daddy's so proud of you, Laine."

She nods, and I press my mouth to hers. She kisses me so gently, squeaking as I move, in and out.

"Let it happen," I tell her. "Take it and it'll feel good, Daddy

promises."

Long slow thrusts, and I won't last long. Her pussy sucks me tight, straining to milk me fucking dry.

My breath is hard and fast as I fight the urge to pound her deep.

And then she whimpers, and this time there's no pain in it. Her hips move under mine, the bed creaking as she grinds back at me.

"*Yes, Daddy,*" she whispers. "*More, Daddy… please, give me more…*"

***

CHAPTER EIGHTEEN

Laine

Daddy is inside me, and it hurts. It hurt enough to take my breath when he pushed all the way in, but I love it, I love the way it feels.

Daddy's big cock makes me feel so tender, but I want it. I want all of him.

"*More, Daddy…*" I whisper. "*Please… please, more…*"

He likes that. He likes it when I beg. He grunts, and kisses me, and his tongue is fierce and wet. My body has a mind of its own, wriggling under him like I know what I'm doing. My pussy wants to take him, my hips rolling from the bed to meet his thrusts, and it feels good under the pain.

"*Yes, Daddy! Like that! Like that!*"

He moves faster, harder, and I hold my breath. He's so deep. I can feel his balls slapping against my ass, and it makes such a dirty noise.

"You've got a perfect little cunt, Laine," he grunts, and it makes me grind back at him.

I can't think straight, and I guess that must be normal. I'm just a bundle of crazy sensations, just a girl who wants her Daddy's cock. I want nothing else. Just him.

"*Harder, Daddy!*"

I must be crazy to say it, and I moan as he slams his dick in and out. I'm making squelchy noises, and I can smell it, *sex*. Daddy is sweaty and I am too, his hair is clammy as I touch it, his lips salty as they press to mine.

He grunts, in a rhythm, and his balls slap my flesh, his dick so deep and my pussy so sore. I can't stop smiling.

I'm not a virgin anymore.

I'm a big girl now. A big girl taking Daddy's nice big dick. A woman. I'm a woman.

He shifts on top of me and it changes everything.

"*Ah...*" I groan. "*Yes...*"

A pressure inside, and a tingle.

"That's it..." he whispers. "That feels so nice..."

It does. It feels so nice I can't stand it, squirming and wriggling and panting.

He pulls his dick all the way out and my pussy feels so empty that I moan.

I moan again as he slides back inside.

Over and over. All the way out, and all the way in.

"*Please, Daddy...*" I'm such a mess, a sweaty horny mess.

He circles his hips and it feels amazing. Better than amazing.

"Daddy's going to come inside you," he says, and my heart races. "Daddy's going to fill you up."

"*Yes!*"

He said he'd give me a baby, and the thought makes me shiver happy shivers. I want Daddy Nick to come inside me and make me pregnant. I didn't even know I wanted it, not for a second, but now he's said it I'm so excited I want to explode.

"It's coming, sweetheart. Daddy's cum is coming…"

Yes.

I feel so proud.

He loses control, his thrusts so erratic and desperate, and I'm desperate too. I grip him tight and moan for him, and my pussy wants it all. He keeps his dick inside me, all the way, and I feel him pulsing and jerking. I'm so happy to know I made Daddy Nick come.

"It's all for you," he whispers. "Daddy's cum is all for you."

I nod, and I'm smiling so hard. "Thank you, Daddy."

He doesn't pull out, just collapses onto me as he breathes so fast. I stroke his hair, and my head is spinning, giddy to know that I've really done it.

He's smiling too. He breathes in my damp hair and holds me tight.

"My perfect girl," he whispers. "My perfect, beautiful little girl."

I'm so proud I could burst.

He smooths the hair from my forehead, and nuzzles me, and I hope this never ends, Daddy and me.

The words won't stay quiet. I can't keep them in.

"I love you, Daddy. I really love you."

He sighs, and it's a good sigh. He raises himself enough to look in my eyes, and they are so warm.

"I love you, too," he says.

***

I feel like I'm flying.

He loves me.

And I love him.

It's real. It's all real.

He pulls out so slowly, so gentle now he's come. I try to move but he shakes his head. He kneels between my legs and spreads my pussy with his fingers. I feel so open. Shy, too. I feel so shy.

"You have the prettiest little pussy, Laine. Daddy wants to see you all full up with his cum."

I feel the burn on my cheeks, and I gasp as he slides his finger inside me.

"So tight."

I feel his finger moving around, and then another.

"We're going to have so much fun together, Laine."

I'm already having more fun than I've ever had. I tell him so and he smiles.

"This is only the beginning."

I believe him. I can't wait to see what else Daddy Nick has to show me.

He lowers his mouth and kisses me where it's tender. "Thank you, Laine, for the greatest gift."

"You're welcome, Daddy." I beam as I stare at him, and wonder how I ever lived without him. I wonder how I ever thought my life could mean anything without him in it.

It makes me want to cry, this love I feel. It's so strong, and so beautiful.

He doesn't seem to understand the tears. His eyes are so worried.

"I'm sorry, sweetheart. Does it hurt?"

I shake my head. "No," I tell him. "It's all amazing, I just… my heart feels so full…"

He pulls me into his arms in a beat, and they hold me so tight, my cheek to his chest as the happy tears fall.

"I love you, Laine," he whispers. "You brought me back to life."

"You *gave* me a life."

"Fate," he says, and I smile.

I wonder if he really believes it, like I do.

And then I wonder if I'm pregnant. I wonder if Daddy's cum will give me a baby.

He doesn't seem to be thinking about it, so I don't say anything.

"We'd better get you cleaned up," he says, and I nod. I need a pee and it feels all squelchy down there. I only notice the stain on the bed when I get to my feet.

It's dark pink with splotches of red. Blood. My blood.

I feel sorry for it, but Daddy is smiling. He touches it like it's magic.

"You bled for me," he says. "Such a beautiful gift from a beautiful girl."

I think it's beautiful too, in a weird way.

Kelly Anne would think I was crazy. She'd think the whole thing was crazy. But I can't wait to tell her anyway.

I want to tell her how amazing it feels not to be a virgin anymore. I want to tell her how Daddy Nick loved me so hard.

But first I need to pee.

***

Daddy Nick follows me into the bathroom, he takes my hands as I lower myself to the toilet, as though I need help. My legs are unsteady, but not that unsteady. I wait for him to leave, but he doesn't. He pulls some toilet paper from the roll and presses it between my legs.

There's more blood when he wipes me. He holds the paper so I can see the stain.

"It'll stop soon," he says, but I'm not worried. I'm more worried that I need a pee.

"I need to go," I tell him.

He doesn't move at all. "We have no secrets, remember?"

My cheeks burn at the thought of Daddy Nick watching me pee. Even though he's seen inside me, and felt in there, and his cum is dripping out of me right now, it still feels so icky to pee in front of him.

"No secrets, Laine," he repeats. "Daddy wants to see."

"You want to watch me… *pee*?" I ask him, sure I must be wrong, but he nods.

"Daddy wants to see everything." He puts his hands on my knees and pulls them apart, and I can't go, not while he's watching. A tiny little trickle drips into the toilet, and his eyes are dark again.

I can't believe he wants it, but he does.

I feel so tickly at the thought. Squirmy as he puts his fingers down there and spreads me open.

"Show Daddy, Laine."

"But I…"

"Laine," he says, and it's stern. "No secrets."

I don't want secrets from Daddy. Even if they are icky ones.

I have to close my eyes to pee. It's so hard to make myself go, but once I start I can't stop. It comes out in a stream, splashing into the

water underneath, and I'm sure some of it must go on Daddy's fingers but he doesn't care. It gives me tickles. Strange tickles right the way through me.

"Not so bad, is it?" he asks.

I shake my head. "No, Daddy."

My pee sounds so loud as it lands. My cheeks feel so hot as he stares.

And then I finish, and it's a relief. I reach for the toilet paper but he's there first. He tears some off and wipes me. Daddy Nick wipes my pussy it's the most normal thing in the world.

I shouldn't like it. I'm sure I shouldn't like it. But I do.

"All clean," he tells me, and his eyes are smiling. He kisses me quick before he reaches for the flush, and his cock is hard again as he gets to his feet.

I must look scared as I stare at it, because he laughs as he pulls me up.

"Bedtime," he tells me. "I think my little girl's had more than enough cock for one day."

I'm only half relieved.

***

Nick

Wiping Laine's sweet pussy is only the tip of the iceberg when it comes to the ways I want to take care of my little girl. Now I've had a taste of her secrets I only want more. I want everything from her.

It's beautiful, her willingness to please me even when she thinks

185

I'm being so *icky.*

I love being icky with Laine. Love pushing her boundaries.

I slide into bed beside her, my cock already hard for more, but it won't be tonight. She's taken enough.

She sighs as she snuggles against me, and I kiss her hair. "Goodnight, sweetheart."

"Goodnight, Daddy Nick."

I'm Daddy Nick again, but that's ok. I hold her so tight and she drifts off to sleep so much more quickly than usual. Her breath is quiet but steady, and just being next to her soothes me. I never want to let her go.

I love my sweet little Laine more than I'd have ever imagined. It's more than desperation for a life less lonely than the one I've been living for so long.

It's in her quiet grace. Her sweet smile. Her easy laugh. It's in the way she's so kind, the way she cares for me, looks up to me, the way she appreciates everything I do for her. The way she's so keen to please me. So keen to be mine.

I love Laine because her bad start hasn't made her bitter, or hostile. It hasn't closed her down to love or made her suspicious. She's still a sweet, soft soul with a warm heart.

She's my beautiful girl. The one bright star on a cloudy night.

I drift off to sleep so soundly in her arms.

***

CHAPTER NINETEEN

Laine

I wake up in Daddy Nick's arms. No college. No work. It makes me smile to find him still sleeping.

I'm not a virgin. I'm not a virgin. I'm not a virgin.

I feel different. Squiggly inside.

Happy.

I roll over to face him, and he stirs but doesn't open his eyes. I stare at him, just because I can. It's a guilty pleasure, staring without him knowing. Like I'm spying, chasing secret glances.

He looks so beautiful in the morning light. His dark eyelashes, his perfect shadow of stubble. His strong nose, his cheekbones. His brows are so well shaped, *serious*, even when he's sleeping. The light makes the grey at his temples look so fine, just a smattering, and it doesn't

make him look old, not like Kelly Anne thinks. It makes him look so professional.

"I know you're staring," he says, and his eyes open into mine. "Good morning, sweetheart."

My heart flutters. "Morning, Daddy Nick."

He doesn't move and neither do I. We lay still, just staring, and there's the softest smile on his lips.

"I haven't slept in in such a long time," he tells me, and I can believe it. He's always up so much earlier than me.

I smile. "It's relaxing. All warm and snuggly."

"It's a tight fit, this bed." He stretches out his legs to illustrate, and he's right, it is a tight fit, but I like it that way. I tell him so and he holds me tighter, squeezes me until I giggle, and then his eyes are serious again. "How do you feel, Laine?"

"Good," I say. "Amazing. You made it amazing. Everything I ever dreamed of."

"Your kind words do wonders for a man's ego."

But Daddy Nick doesn't have an ego. He's strong, but not arrogant. I know plenty of arrogant people, I've known them my whole life, the people that think they know everything, that they're cooler than everyone, better than everyone. Better than *me*. I've known so many people who think they're better than me.

But not Daddy Nick.

"Are you hungry, sweetheart?"

I tell him no, because I don't want to move, but my tummy betrays me and rumbles.

"I think you might be a little liar, Laine Seabourne." He taps my nose, and I can't stop laughing. I wonder if it's some kind of weird post-virginity-losing endorphin thing, because my body feels light enough to float away. He throws back the covers and I groan through

the giggles, but he doesn't care. He kisses my forehead before he drops his feet to the floor, and then he's up.

My laughter stops when I see he's hard. A pang between my legs as I remember how he felt there.

He grabs his cock as I stare. "You can't honestly be surprised, sweetheart. I've been in bed with a beautiful, delicious young woman."

Woman.

He called me a woman.

It feels better than I ever thought it would feel.

"Are you getting up with me?" he asks, and I nod. Even though the sheets have embraced me as one of their own, I still want to get up with him. I hold out my hand like a lazy cow as I yawn, and he pulls me up. I can feel the difference when I get to my feet, my pussy so tender, and my legs wobbly.

"All alright?" he asks. He takes my pink robe from the door and helps me into it.

"I'm good," I say. "I'm just… I feel different…"

"You feel like you've been fucked," he says. "You'll get used to that, sweetheart."

I follow him as he steps out onto the landing, keeping to his side like a shadow. I follow him into the bathroom without a thought, and he smiles a sly smile.

"Wanting to return the favour?" I look blankly until his smile turns into a smirk. "Daddy needs to take a piss, Laine." My cheeks burn, and I say I'm sorry, but he grabs my hand. "I didn't mean you should leave. You don't need to leave, sweetheart. Not if you don't want to. No secrets, remember?"

I've never seen a man pee before. The thought excites me, even though it might be icky. I can't even imagine what Kelly Anne would say.

189

He steps over to the toilet and lifts the seat, and his cock is in his hand, still a little hard as he aims at the bowl. I step closer, and my mouth is dry. It feels dirty. *Nice* dirty.

The stream comes out so fast when it starts, and it must feel good, because he closes his eyes and lets out a groan. I'm still staring when he opens them, and he's smirking again. I feel like such a silly idiot, and maybe he knows, because he tips his head and beckons me closer.

"Don't be shy," he tells me.

He takes my hand and I jump a little as he wraps my fingers around his dick. I'm not expecting him to let go, but he does. His cock jerks and makes me start, and pee sprays off the side of the bowl like crazy. He laughs. "Steady, sweetheart."

I'm sure this isn't what other people do, but I'm transfixed. It half makes me want to giggle and half makes my clit tingle, and I'm positive that must make me a dirty girl, not the little prude Kelly Anne has me down for. That makes me strangely proud. Strangely grown up. Kelly Anne tells me everything about her sex life, and there's never been anything like this. But then again, there's never been so much of anything Daddy Nick has shown me. Nobody's ever put their tongue in Kelly Anne's asshole and told her how good it tastes. She'd *definitely* have told me about that. She'd have bragged for a month.

It's ridiculously fun, aiming someone else's pee around the bowl. His cock feels different like this, only half hard. He's still big and veiny, but less… *threatening*. I dunno if threatening is the right word, but it'll do.

The spray eases to a trickle, and then just a drip, and I wonder what I should do next. Maybe shake him, or wipe him? I don't have a clue. I squeeze him instead, and it takes him by surprise. He grunts, and shifts on his feet, and there's a thrill right through me as I feel him swell in my grip.

"Dirty girl," he says, and I'm beginning to believe it. My pussy clenches and it feels different than usual… tender, and achy, and…

horny. I keep squeezing, moving my hand up and down him with the sweetest smile on my face I can manage, and he likes that too. He can't stop looking at me.

His hand tightens around mine, and he moves me harder, faster.

"Want to jerk Daddy off in the bathroom? Is that what my dirty little girl wants?"

I nod. I do want that.

I feel more in control than I've ever felt around him, wrapped up tight in a fluffy robe while he stands naked, his dick in my hand. I've been learning, trying really hard to do it just as he likes it, and it's working. His breath is fast, and the muscles in his thighs are so tight, his eyes staring at my fingers as they work so hard.

"That's so good," he groans. "That's really good, Laine."

I don't feel so much like his little girl this morning. I'm a woman, not a prudish little virgin. I'm the one giving him all the pleasure as he thrusts in my grip.

"You want to make me come? Like this?"

"Yes." My voice sounds more confident than usual.

His eyes meet mine, and I smile but don't add a *please* or a *Daddy* or even a *Daddy Nick*. I can tell he's thinking about it, I can see it in his eyes, but he doesn't say anything and I take it as some kind of silly victory. I can't explain why, it just is.

Not being a virgin anymore has definitely gone to my head.

I nearly snort giggle at the thought of me in slutty underwear and ridiculously high heels as I morph into some sex siren, but when he arches his back and his cock twitches, everything becomes so serious.

I'm going to make him come, without his help, without him taking over, or putting it in my mouth, or gripping my fingers and showing me what to do.

"Fuck, Laine," he groans. "That's so fucking nice."

My heart swells with pride, knowing I can do this. I'm not such the silly little prude I thought I was.

My wrist is aching but I don't slow down, I concentrate on the tip of him, where he's getting wet, and that makes him grunt and sway and curse. I love the way it makes him curse.

"Fuck, I'm close," he tells me, but I already know that, I can feel it in the way his cock jerks, in the rasp of his breath.

I could explode with joy when the first spurt of cum splatters the cistern. It's not even close to the bowl, but that doesn't matter, Daddy Nick isn't even looking. His eyes are screwed shut, his voice nothing more than grunts as he spurts again and again.

I made him come.

A milestone that seems like such a big deal.

I can't stop grinning.

"You look like the cat who got the cream," he laughs when he's gathered his breath. "Well done, sweetheart. That was perfect."

Perfect.

My cheeks tickle from smiling so bright. "Thanks."

"I'll be expecting that kind of treatment every morning, if you're not careful," he says, but he's joking, his eyes sparkle. "Now, let's go and get you some breakfast, you've certainly earned it."

He slaps my ass as he passes me by, and grins as he grabs his robe.

***

This isn't the morning Daddy Nick I've come to know. He makes breakfast and hums a song I've never heard. He's relaxed today. Today I help him, chopping up mushrooms as he fries the sausages, and

getting the bread ready for the toaster.

"Teamwork," he says as I drop the mushrooms into the pan.

"Teamwork," I agree, and raise myself on tiptoes until he presses his lips to mine.

The bacon smells incredible, and I really am ravenous. I let out the most contented sigh as we sit down to eat our meal, and he smiles over at me before he tucks in.

"I used to hate the weekends," he tells me. "They felt so empty. I'd work, just to fill the time."

"Mine too," I admit. "I mean I babysat, but Kelly Anne is normally busy in the daytime, and Mum would be out. Crappy TV was my friend."

"Crosswords were mine," he admits. "When the to-do list was checked off, that is."

The bacon tastes as delicious as it smells. I tell him so and he compliments me on how the mushrooms are sliced just so.

"So, here we are," he says. "A whole weekend with no work, and no babysitting. What to do, Laine?"

I shrug. "Whatever you want. I'm happy just being here with you."

"And I'm happy being here with you," he says. "But we should go out, do something, live a little."

I've been living plenty, but I don't tell him that. I get the feeling he's really breathing for the first time in forever, and I get that, because I am too. Like a butterfly breaking out of a lonely cocoon. That's what I feel like.

Like a butterfly.

Butterflies.

I have an idea. A great idea that gives me shivers.

"What?" he asks. "Where do you want to go?"

I shrug like it's nothing. "Just somewhere. I need to look it up online."

"We'll go wherever you want," he says. "My treat."

But not today. Today will be *my* treat.

I keep quiet and eat my breakfast, and he does too. He looks at me curiously, as though he's trying to read me, but I keep a poker face, determined not to ruin the surprise. I so want to surprise him.

I clear our plates as soon as we're done.

***

CHAPTER TWENTY

Nick

She's bursting to tell me where we're headed, clutching her phone so tightly as she relays the directions from the navigation software. Her voice bubbles with excitement. *A surprise*, she insists.

I can't remember a time someone gave me a surprise like this. Not even Louisa. Louisa was sweet and vivacious, but she wasn't thoughtful. I enjoyed spoiling Louisa, just as I enjoy spoiling my little Laine, but the creature in the seat beside me is turning out to be a very different girl altogether.

"Don't I get a clue?" I ask.

Her hair shimmers as she shakes her head. "No. You'll like it, though. At least I hope you will."

I'm already liking it. Being with her is enjoyment enough all on its own.

I keep my eyes on the road, none the wiser of our destination as I take the roads she points out.

"Not far," she says. "Take a right, up here."

And that's when I see it. A brown tourist sign on the roadside. *Butterfly Zoo.*

"Crap." She groans. "I didn't know that would be there. I wanted it to be a surprise."

But it *is* a surprise. It's such a surprise I'm lost for words. I was just a boy when I last took my net and disappeared into the countryside to indulge my fascination with butterflies.

Now I only admire them dead. So many lifeless specimens, pinned and mounted in frames on my wall.

The excitement in my stomach is boyish and unfamiliar. An innocence long since forgotten. Buried, with the rest of my life.

"You do want to go, right?" she asks. "You do still like them?"

"I love them," I tell her, and my heart pounds with the thrill as we pull into the car park.

I park up in a space and turn off the engine, then sit, staring in wonder at the bright painted wings over the entrance doors.

I want to tell her how strange I feel inside, how her thoughtfulness has moved me to nothing but stunted silence, but it's all I can do to smile and take her hand in mine.

Her fingers squeeze. "They've got over two hundred species here. Some rare ones, too. I looked it up online."

"This is really something, Laine," I tell her.

"So, let's go," she says. "Show me some butterflies. I can't wait to see."

Neither can I.

We check in at the entrance, and as I pay the fee I ramble on to the attendant with an enthusiasm so alien. I hand Laine the complimentary spotter pamphlet with a smile.

I won't need it. I know so many by heart.

The place isn't busy, not on a cold December morning. The crowds are sparse, even though the glass ceilings bathe us in beautiful warm sunlight. We enter the main butterfly dome unhindered by queues.

A mass of exotic plants. Colour and life and beating wings. Thousands upon thousands of butterflies that overload my senses. I gawp, like an imbecile, so taken by the sight that my breath catches in my throat.

"This is amazing!" she says, and it's all I can do to nod.

An emerald and black butterfly takes lazy flight in front of us, its wings big and shimmering with metallic beauty. Laine frantically thumbs through the spotter guide, but I still her with a squeeze of my hand on her shoulder.

"Papilio blumei," I tell her. "Found only on the Indonesian island of Sulawesi. It's a peacock, otherwise known as a green swallowtail."

"It's beautiful," she says, and her eyes follow it all the way out of sight.

"I've got one on the wall."

"I've seen it." She smiles. "But it's so much more beautiful when it's flying, don't you think?"

I'm sure there's no deeper meaning intended behind her words, but I feel it nonetheless.

"Yes, Laine. It's so much more beautiful alive."

"*I* feel alive," she tells me.

"Me too, sweetheart. Me too."

I wander amongst the plants, leading Laine so gently along the paths marked out. So many butterflies, and I tell her about them all. I tell her their Latin names and where they're from. I tell her if they're endangered, and what sizes they grow to.

She listens in wonder, hanging onto every word I say. I think she

may love them nearly as much as I do.

Her steps are light and bouncy, her gasps genuine. "That one!" she squeals, pointing up ahead. "It's so beautiful!"

And it is.

Of course it is.

The Maculinea Arion is the largest and rarest of the blue English butterflies. Little, blue-eyed Laine reminds me of one – so beautiful in her fragility. So graceful and delicate. Such a rare delight. I tell her so, and her smile melts my heart.

"That's really nice."

"And really true, sweetheart."

The Arion flutters close, and my breath hitches, the thrill palpable. I see the butterfly's path, see so clearly that it's going to land. It couldn't be more perfect, and it makes me shiver. *Fate*, she would say, and I'm beginning to believe her. I step away and take out my phone, just quickly enough to call up my camera app.

The butterfly dithers around her head before it lands, perches and flaps its wings once, twice, three times before it rests, so blue against Laine's pale blonde hair. I watch my beautiful girl crowned by the beautiful butterfly, my heart full to bursting as so many others flutter around us.

Her shock is divine, her expression of wonder so beautifully innocent, and I know it for certain. Laine will love butterflies as much as I do. I can see it in her eyes.

I capture the moment and I know it's one I will savour forever.

***

Talk is so easy on the way home. Laine flicks through the spotter

pamphlet as though it's a treasured possession, reading me out the names in Latin to make sure she has the pronunciation right. Her sweet voice makes them ethereal. Magical.

Wonderful.

"Maybe you could teach me how to spot them in the wild," she says. "It sounds fun."

"Harder work than the zoo." I smile to myself. "It's a different kind of fun, Laine, but no less enjoyable."

"I think I'd like it," she tells me, and I do too.

A few weeks ago I'd have struggled to ever imagine myself trekking into the countryside with jars and nets, but not today. Today anything feels possible.

"Better than crosswords, right?" she asks.

That makes me laugh. "Yes, Laine, considerably better than crosswords."

"Better than TV, too," she says.

We stop for dinner at a fancy little restaurant on the outskirts of the city, and I stare at her as she scours the menu.

"I don't know what to choose," she admits. "I don't know what half this stuff is."

I slide my chair around to her side of the table and talk her through the options. Her hand rests on my knee under the tablecloth and squeezes, and she's so close, so intoxicatingly close. I can smell her shampoo, and *her*, close enough to enjoy the flutter of her eyelashes as her eyes wander over the main courses.

"I think we should go with the winter roast," I tell her.

She nods. "That sounds good to me."

I move back to my own side of the table before I give our order to the waiter, and already I'm missing her touch.

"When did you know you first liked butterflies?" she asks, and it makes me smile to realise she's still thinking about them.

"A school project," I tell her. "Infant school, I must've been only five or six. A conservation assignment, *British wildlife and its habitat*. We went out into the meadow behind the school and I spotted a monarch fluttering from leaf to leaf. I was mesmerised by its colours. Once I started watching them I never stopped. My father bought me a net for my birthday, I didn't even ask. It was a surprise."

"That was nice of him, to encourage that."

"He was a fair man. Stern, but fair," I tell her.

"Stern," she repeats with a smile, and I know exactly what she's thinking.

She's picturing my father's belt on my backside, the severity of the punishment I received in his old study.

"As I said, stern but fair." I pour her a mineral water from the jug on the table. "As I hope to be. That's what I aim for, Laine, that same balance."

"I haven't seen you stern. Not yet."

I hand her the glass. "You will, given time. When it's necessary, sweetheart, only when it's necessary."

"I'll always be good, Da-" Her voice falters, and I get it. She's unsure how to address me in public. Daddy Nick sounds so fucking creepy.

Perverse and *icky*, as Laine would call it. Because it is. It is icky.

Dirty.

It's fucking dirty.

But my cock's already hard at the thought.

I don't care who hears us in this place, and that's a new feeling too, the disregard for appearances. My professional conduct is the only thing in recent years I've had to concern myself with, and that's for my

father's legacy and the firm's reputation rather than anything personal.

"It's *Daddy*, sweetheart," I tell her.

She looks uncertain, her cheeks flushing. "In public? I thought this was…"

"You thought it was at home only?" I raise an eyebrow. "Is that what you want?"

She shakes her head but she doesn't seem entirely sure. "You said people wouldn't understand… people like Kelly Anne…"

"And they wouldn't. The complexity is too confusing." I lean closer. "In this place I can be your daddy or your lover. Or both." I smirk. "It depends how devilish you feel."

I'm joking, but her eyes tell me she isn't. They flash with dark amusement, and she wants it. I know she wants it.

Interesting.

My sweet little Laine is certainly interesting.

"I'll call you Daddy," she whispers.

***

Laine

I'm burning up as the waiter brings our meal. This is new ground, him being Daddy here, around people. It makes it seem so real and so tingly.

The waiter smiles as he places my plate in front of me, and I wonder if I should find a way to say it aloud. I wonder if that's what Daddy Nick wants.

He doesn't give me an opportunity to find a way. He does it for me.

"Doesn't that look lovely, sweetheart?" he asks. The waiter looks at me, waits for a reaction with a smile.

My heart is racing. "Yes… it does, Daddy."

Daddy Nick smiles so bright, and I feel like I've passed a test. I like it. I really like it.

"It looks really yummy, Daddy," I say, trying it out some more. It comes so much easier than I thought it would.

I wonder how old the waiter thinks I am. Fifteen, maybe sixteen at most. Just the right age to have a daddy like Nick.

"Enjoy your meal," the waiter says, and leaves us, just like that. As though it's the most normal thing in the world, a little girl eating out with her daddy on a Saturday evening.

"Good girl," Daddy Nick says, and I feel it in my tummy.

"I don't look much like you," I whisper.

"Then I guess you look like your mother." His eyes twinkle so darkly, and I wonder if he's hard. I wish I could find out.

Dinner tastes really good, but I hardly want to eat a thing. I have to force it down, but my thighs are doing that clenching thing they do, and I'm squirming on my seat, hoping Daddy Nick will take me again when we get home. Hoping he'll do it fast and hard and make those horny grunts he makes when he loses control.

"Eat up," he tells me. "You'll need the energy when we get home."

I eat every single bite.

***

CHAPTER TWENTY ONE

Nick

I drive faster than usual, my dick straining in my lap, so fucking hard at the thought of thrusting into Laine's tight little pussy.

She doesn't speak, just stares at the road ahead. But she's fidgety, her cute little ass shuffling in the passenger seat. I know I'll find her knickers nice and wet for me, the thought makes my mouth water.

"You can touch yourself," I tell her. "It's dark. No one can see inside the car."

I feel her wide eyes on me. Such delicious shock. "But I…"

"But you what?"

"I don't know…" she admits. "It feels…"

"*Dirty*," I tell her. "*Daddy's* feeling dirty right now, sweetheart. Daddy wants to take his little girl home and bury his cock in her pretty little cunt."

A pause, and then I hear the zipper on her jeans.

"Good girl." My balls tighten. "Make yourself nice and wet for Daddy. Tell him how it feels."

I can see her little hand rubbing from the corner of my eye. "It feels… *ah*… it feels…"

"Play with that sweet little clit, Laine, but don't come. You come only for Daddy."

"*Ah… but I'm so…*"

"Only Daddy makes you come, Laine. Understood?" My voice is so harsh, laced with the pressure of my straining fucking cock.

"*Yes, Daddy…*" Her hand slows down its rubbing.

We're turning onto our street before I know it, and Laine keeps rubbing herself right until I turn off the engine. She piles out of the car without fastening up her jeans, and they're so easy to yank down her thighs once we make it into the kitchen. I press into her from behind and walk her forward with frantic steps until I've pinned her against the kitchen island, her tiny body so delicious as I grind against her ass, my fingers snaking around to slip inside her knickers and rub at her needy little clit.

"You're so fucking wet for Daddy," I hiss. "So fucking wet."

I dip my fingertips in her slit to illustrate, and she moans for me.

"You want Daddy's cock again, don't you?" My mouth is right by her ear. "Tell Daddy how much you want his cock."

"*Please, Daddy!*" she cries. "*I want it so much!*"

"Say it."

"*I want your cock, Daddy! Fuck me!*"

She's learning.

The ache in my groin is more than I can fucking bear. I spin her around me and hitch her up onto the granite, tugging down her wet knickers and spreading her thighs nice and wide. Her pink slit is puffy and glistening, mine for the fucking taking as I spit on my fingers and

sink two all the way inside.

She moans a delightful little moan, and I fuck her harder, my fingers easing and stretching her open. She's still so tight, her tiny hole such a fucking wonder. "*Yes! Yes, Daddy!*"

I move in circles, nice and deep, applying pressure until she gasps. I groan for her as I clamp my mouth onto her pretty little mound, and her clit is so easy to find, standing proud for my tongue.

She bucks her hips, urging me deeper, and I suck, flicking my tongue so quickly over that hard little bud.

"*Daddy!*" Her voice is breathless, frantic. "*I'm gonna come, Daddy!*"

I stare up at my gorgeous girl, her cheeks flushed and lips parted. Her top has ridden up to her bra, her tummy so tight. Her legs wrap around my shoulders, and she uses them as leverage, rubbing her pussy against my face as she shudders. She loses control, cursing in such a pretty little voice, and I keep on lapping until she's all used up.

Her wetness is in my nostrils, smeared slick over my mouth. She tastes fucking divine. I get to my feet when she's done, and take out my cock, spearing her so suddenly that she squeals.

"*Ow, ow, ow...*" she groans as I push all the way inside. She rocks her hips regardless as her pussy takes me, and her mouth is open wide for my kisses. Her hands reach around to grab my ass, and my horny little girl urges me on, urges *harder, faster*.

Her innocence hides such a dirty little minx, just begging to be coaxed out into the open.

I shouldn't come without using protection, not without a serious discussion, but my sweet little Laine surprises me yet again.

"*Come, Daddy! I want it! I want it in me!*"

And so do I.

I want to fill that tight little cunt with my seed, I want to fill her up until she's swollen with my child, and her pretty little tits are so ripe.

It's the beast within, I know it. I feel it behind my eyes, the desire to claim her forever. It's all kinds of fucking wrong, but I can't resist.

Frantic thrusts and I unload, her sweet cunt sucks it from me, milking my balls until they run dry.

She drips as I pull out of her, and her freshly fucked hole is a sight straight from heaven.

She catches her breath, smiling as I run a thumb over her slit.

"Such a good girl for Daddy," I tell her. "All full up."

Her eyes twinkle as she tugs her crumpled top over her head.

"I want more," she says.

***

Laine

Daddy Nick loves me all through Saturday night. He loves me until I'm too sore to take his cock anymore, and then takes me with his mouth instead.

Daddy Nick loves me until we're both panting and sweaty. He loves me until there are no words, only breath.

He loves me until I fall asleep in his arms, and then he wakes and loves me again on a bright Sunday morning.

We eat toast, and then he bathes me. He washes my hair, and soaps me all over, and then he pushes his fingers inside my ass. Only this time it makes me so horny I beg him to love me all over again.

He does.

He gives me so much.

He gives me everything, over and over through Sunday night.

He's still taking me as the birds are chirping outside, and I'm too scared to check my phone alarm, knowing my sleep will be barely enough to function.

It isn't.

I don't want to wake up for college. I barely move as I hear his voice from downstairs. My head feels muggy and my pussy feels sore, and all I want to do is curl up with him and talk about butterflies, but Daddy Nick doesn't do days off.

He's already dressed so smart for work. Already cooking my breakfast.

I eat slowly, my eyes still heavy with sleep, and he smiles and calls me lazybones, then leaves me to clear our plates as he finishes getting ready to leave.

I startle as he claps his hands in front of my face, and I'm still in the same position at the table, my breakfast plate still empty in front of me.

"Chop-chop, sweetheart, we're late. We can't be late, Laine."

His voice is stern and filled with irritation, and I feel mortified to have disappointed him in such a silly way. I rush to my feet and clear the plates with a clatter, then bound upstairs two steps at a time to brush my teeth and gather my messy hair into a ponytail. I throw on my clothes, still fastening my jeans as I race to the door while he's waiting. I barely notice the lunchbox he thrusts in my hands, and follow him out to the car in a daze.

The frosty air wakes me up enough to attempt conversation, but he's still irritated, checking the clock on the dashboard every few seconds.

"I'm sorry, Daddy," I say.

"An early night for you, young lady," he tells me. I don't disagree.

I could sleep for ten years straight.

I'm groggy when Kelly Anne catches me in the corridor. She's grinning, bursting to tell me some stupid news or other. It's about a guy, not *Harrison*, some other stupid *stud* called Mason she met down the fish and chip shop. *Mason*. I doubt that's even his real name. She tells me he's built like a bear, and fucks like one, too.

The way she talks about him you'd think he was the master of the female orgasm, but she's full of shit, I can see that now.

I wonder if she's always been so full of shit.

Probably.

She rolls her eyes. "You don't seem all that interested. I guess *Daddy Nick* is sooo much more important than *me* now…" She follows me anyway. "So, have you *actually* fucked the guy yet?"

She clearly doesn't believe for one second I've done it. I shouldn't rise to the bait, but she's been looking at me like such a prude for so long now that I can't help but revel in the fact that I'm not.

I stop walking, and even though I'm exhausted and still so gutted I upset Daddy Nick this morning, there's still a sizzle all the way through me.

"Yes," I tell her. "I *have*. And it was great. It was amazing. *He* was amazing." I grin, and once it's on my face it won't leave.

She looks so shocked, her eyes so wide as she gawps at me.

"Wow," she says. "Congratulations." It's hollow and empty. Her insincerity is so obvious now I have Nick in my life.

Nick. I haven't thought of him with just his actual name for days.

"I love him," I tell her, and I'm so confident with the statement it takes me aback. "I love him and he loves me, and it's amazing."

She shrugs. "Yeah, well, I thought that about *my* first shag, too. You'll get over it."

I shake my head. "It's different."

"Oh yeah? How would *you* know?"

There's a million reasons I'd know. The way he looks at me, the way he cares, the way he holds me and kisses me and his eyes turn so dark when he wants me. The way he breathes so steadily when he's sleeping next to me. The way he speaks with me, shares things with me, the way he's so tender when he brushes my hair.

"I just know," I tell her, and there's that confidence again. I've never been confident before. It feels so weird.

"So, what you gonna do now? Get knocked up and have two-point-four kids and live happily ever after in his fancy house?"

The thought of that makes me feel so tickly inside. "Maybe."

She looks at me like I'm an idiot. A real idiot. "Jesus, Laine. What's wrong with you? You want to have *kids* with creepy guy?"

"He's not creepy."

"He's *so* fucking creepy. Buying you a phone and making your sandwiches, dressing you up sweet in your cute little pastel clothes."

I look down at my outfit. "What's wrong with my clothes?"

"Urgh. *Nothing*." She rolls her eyes again. "I'm just worried, alright? You're so weird lately."

Happy. I think the word is *happy*. It's on the tip of my tongue to tell her, but as usual she's done with talking about me. "He does know you're coming out for my birthday, right?"

My heart drops at the revelation. Kelly Anne's birthday. I calculate the date. *Saturday*. The thought pains.

"I, um… I didn't know we were…"

She looks genuinely hurt. "You're not coming?! For real? Like we don't *always* go out on my fucking birthday!"

I wouldn't call it that. A couple down her local pub where they

knew we were underage but didn't care.

"We can go," I say. "Just for a few, like normal."

She groans. "No way, Laine! Clubbing on the beachfront. There's a drum and bass night I want to check out." My stomach lurches at the thought, and she must see the horror. "I said I was sorry! You can keep hold of your own shit this time if you're so worried."

I want to say no, want to tell her to go out with some of her fake Facebook friends instead. The ones who like her comments but don't give a shit about her in real life.

"You'd have more fun with other people, Kels. I'm not really up for drinking that much."

Her frown makes me feel so guilty. "But *you're* my *best* friend! I want you to meet Mason! Please, Laine! Jeez, do you want me to fucking beg or something? I said I'm sorry about last time, what else do you want?" Class is about to start, but she folds her arms and makes no move to leave. "Please, Laine! Say you'll come!"

I'm so cornered. Cornered and guilty.

"I'll talk to Nick…"

"You need his *permission* now?!"

"No," I say. And I don't. I'm sure I don't. Even though I'm also sure I do.

"So you'll come, then?"

I'm trapped. Her eyes pleading and her shoulders so rigid. I'm trapped into going out for her birthday, because she's been my friend for as long as I can remember.

"Alright," I say. "I'll come. But only for a few, okay? Just for a few!"

She grins, triumphant, then slings her arm around my shoulder as we head for class.

All I feel is dread.

CHAPTER TWENTY TWO

Nick

I'm more tired than I can remember. Amusing though it is, I should be far too sensible to indulge in a crazy weekend of fucking on such little sleep. Still, I feel sated. Thoroughly sated.

I feel blessed. Calm.

Loved.

A tap on my door, and my bright-eyed assistant steps in. She looks considerably fresher than I feel.

"Morning, Penny," I offer, and my tiredness fades into the background as I notice the box in her hands.

"Morning, Mr Lynch." Her smile is nervous. "I picked out that gift you wanted. Charged it to your expenses account on the weekend. I hope that's okay," she dithers in front of my desk, so unsure. "It was expensive…"

I wave her concerns aside. "That's great, Penny. Thank you."

211

She sighs, pretends to wipe her brow. And then she hands it over.

The box is black leather with fine embossed lettering. It opens so smoothly in my hands.

Penny stares at me as I stare at the gift she's chosen. It's beautiful. A perfect heart, so tasteful in its simplicity, twinkling with a delicate pink stone as an accent.

"It's platinum," she says. "And that's a real diamond…"

"An excellent choice."

"I'm glad you like it."

I close the box, and meet her smile. "Thank you, Penny."

She hovers, and I stay quiet as she plucks up whatever courage she's summoning. "Will she like it?"

"I hope so," I say.

"She's a lucky girl."

"I'm sure she'll appreciate such a beautiful gift." I wait for it, interested to see how bold she is with her questioning.

She keeps her eyes on the box. "Will she wear it to the Christmas party?"

The Christmas party.

I've barely given it a thought. It's been merely a duty up until now. My attendance a necessary annoyance as senior partner of the practice.

I imagine Laine on my arm this year, and the prospect is considerably more appealing.

"I would think so, Penny."

Her eyes are so warm. "That's great. What's her name?"

"Laine," I say.

"*Laine*," she repeats. "I look forward to meeting her."

"I'm sure she'll enjoy meeting you, too."

She makes to leave, but I call her back. "One more thing, Penny, if you will."

"Of course."

I open the gallery app on my phone and ping a copy of the butterfly picture to her inbox as she waits. "I've emailed you an image. I'd like it printed, please, a frame, too. I know you'll find something just perfect."

"I'll do my best, Mr Lynch."

I'm sure she will.

My phone tells me it's almost lunchtime as I drop it back onto my desk.

I've just time to finish up my current report before it's time to call Laine.

***

Laine

Kelly Anne doesn't bother speaking as we sit in the canteen. She knows the routine by now, knows he'll be calling me any minute.

I dig in my bag for my phone, just like always. I like to be prepared for when his call comes in.

Only my phone isn't in my bag this morning.

I root around, as though searching all the harder will make it materialise out of thin air.

Kelly Anne sighs as she watches. "Left your fancy phone at home, did you? Daddy Nick's gonna be pissed you're not at his beck and call."

She has no idea.

I feel like such an ass for sleeping in and rushing so fast to make it up to him. I can imagine exactly where my phone is, still plugged in at the side of the bed, probably still chirping out the alarm that I snoozed ten times this morning. *Shit.*

I feel myself pale, my mouth dry as paper.

"Chill, Laine, it's just a phone. No big deal."

But it is a big deal. He always calls at one on the dot. He likes to get hold of me, to check I'm okay.

"He always calls…" I begin, like she has a hope of hell of understanding.

"So?"

"So, he always calls. It's important."

She tuts at me. "*So important.* I'm sure he can wait a few hours for a status update on how yummy your sandwich was."

I wish I could explain, but there's no way I will. I wish I could tell her how worried he'll be, how much tragedy he's been through. I wish I could tell her that keeping me safe is everything to Daddy Nick.

I try to figure a way to get hold of him, but the idea of calling him at the office practically brings on a panic attack. What would I even say? And would he be angry?

More angry than he'll be at me for forgetting my phone?

I probably already made him late this morning, and now this. I feel like such an idiot.

Maybe he'll punish me.

The thought is right there, and so is the guilty flutter between my legs.

I shouldn't want that. Definitely shouldn't want him to be mad with me. *Disappointed* in me.

I wonder if he'll use the belt his father used on him. I wonder how

much it'll hurt.

Maybe he won't.

Maybe he'll brush it off and tell me to be more careful next time.

I doubt it. And I'm not sure that's such a bad thing.

"Chill, Laine, you look like you've seen a fucking ghost." Kelly Anne sighs and takes a swig of her drink.

The nerves are dancing in my tummy, and the tickles tickle between my legs. I feel sick, hot and cold and tingly all at once.

"I shouldn't have forgotten my phone," I say.

But Kelly Anne doesn't care at all.

***

Nick

I call again. And again after that.

I stare at my phone screen and breathe through the irrational nerves.

Maybe she's been held up in class. Maybe she's in a noisy canteen.

It happens.

I'm fooling myself. It's part of the rules, our lunchtime phone call. She always answers on the second ring. Like clockwork.

Only not today.

I consider my options, contemplating calling the college reception and leaving a message for her, but what would be the point?

I'll look like a stalker for the sake of easing my paranoia, that or alarm her unnecessarily.

I force myself to get a grip, to reflect on the morning and weigh up the situation rationally.

She was tired and rushed, barely awake when I dropped her off at college. There's almost certainly an entirely innocent explanation.

Almost certainly.

If there is then I shall punish her for breaking the rules so carelessly, and if there isn't…

I daren't even give that a thought.

I struggle through my afternoon appointments, endeavouring to give my clients my professional attention with my nerves wound tight in my chest.

I try Laine's phone again during a lull in meetings. It rings through to voicemail just as Michael French steps into my room. He's my joint senior partner, as much of a friend as I'd class anyone, not that the bar's particularly high.

His smile tells me he's heard the news. I wouldn't have imagined anything less, not now I've given Penny gossip-worthy detail. I didn't expect the news would stay a secret, and I'm sure Penny didn't consider it confidential information, not now I'm officially bringing my partner to the Christmas party.

"Tell me about Laine with the pink diamond," Mike says and holds out his hand across the desk. "Congratulations on the couple status."

I shake it warmly. "Word travels fast…"

"Secretaries talk." He tips his head. "She must be quite a woman to snare a stoic old dog like you."

"Enough of the old." I laugh a professional laugh, even though it feels like rusty iron in my throat.

"So," he prompts. "What's she like? You kept that one close to your chest."

I cast another glance at my phone before I answer. No messages. "She's sweet and kind. Gracious. Beautiful."

"Blonde?"

I smile. "Blonde, yes."

"Nice legs?"

I meet his stare. "Nice smile. A nice heart. The legs are merely a bonus, Mike."

"So she *does* have nice legs…" He laughs to himself. "Can't wait to meet her. I'm sure Barbara will love getting to know her."

Barbara French celebrated her fiftieth birthday last summer. She's a wildfire, a sharp cracker with a sharp tongue and absolutely nothing in common with little Laine.

Mike's digging and I know it. I make him wait, pretending to check out a fresh email.

I use the moment to contemplate whether I'm ready for this, but it doesn't take all that long to consider.

I'm ready for everything Laine brings to my life, including any awkward questions.

I take a breath. "She's eighteen, Mike." I hold his stare without flinching.

He doesn't flinch either. "A sweet young thing, I'm sure."

"Very."

"Then I'm happy for you." His smile is genuine enough. "We should go out one night, celebrate with some champagne. Introduce young Laine to our office family."

"She'll be coming to the Christmas party," I tell him, like he hasn't already heard.

"Excellent. I'll be bringing Caroline, she's back from university and no doubt she'll be bored enough to come along. I'm sure they'll get on

fantastically. Maybe they could spend some time together. Caroline gets lonely without her uni pals. You know how it is when you're that age."

I'm not sure I remember, but smile regardless. "I'm sure Laine would enjoy that," I tell him.

"Excellent," he says. "I look forward to meeting the future Mrs Lynch."

I raise my eyebrows. "That's quite a statement."

"She must be quite a woman," he says again. "Any woman that can catch your heart after all these years has got to be one to keep hold of." He tips his head at me. "I'll get Barbara to pick out a hat ready for the big day."

"You do that," I say.

He thinks I'm joking, I'm sure, and on some level I am. Making polite conversation for the sake of appearances. But it's more than that.

She's becoming a part of my life.

It feels beautiful, and that only makes me worry all the more.

I try her phone again.

***

Laine

I rush out through the college gates, sighing in relief to find his car in the usual spot. I throw myself into the passenger seat, full of sorry explanations.

I'm an idiot! I forgot my phone! I rushed out and left it there, right there by the bedside table! I'm so sorry. I'm an idiot. I'm an idiot. I'm an

idiot.

He doesn't say a word, just reverses the Mercedes out of the space and heads for home.

I don't know what else I can say, so I say nothing, just tap my fingers on my lunchbox.

I wish he'd go crazy and tell me how angry he is, just to get it over with, but he doesn't.

"I was worried," he says, so simply.

"I know," I tell him. "I get it. I get how worried you'd be. I'm really sorry."

"Rushing is a fool's errand, Laine. Carelessness leads nowhere good."

I tell him I know that, too. Tell him I'm sorry again.

He says nothing else, just stares at the road ahead.

I hate how it feels to disappoint him.

He pulls onto our driveway and parks up as usual. He opens the front door and steps inside as usual. Hangs his jacket up as usual.

And then he heads through to the sitting room. I follow him, hoping that maybe he'll break the ice and tell me about his day, but he doesn't.

He unfastens his cufflinks as I watch, and rolls his cuffs back.

My heart races, and I'm not even sure why. I just know that something's brewing.

That tickle between my legs again, but it's faint under the nerves.

"Naughty girls need discipline, sweetheart. I told you what happens when you disregard the rules."

"Yes, Daddy," I whisper. "I'm sorry, Daddy."

"I'm sure you are," he tells me and his voice is stern again, like it

was when I was late this morning. "But sorry alone isn't enough to learn your lesson, Laine. The rules are there for a reason, to keep you safe."

"I know, Daddy…" I feel so young again. Young and ditzy and awkward, barely like the horny little cow who took his cock all weekend.

"You know that I have to do this."

I nod, because I do know, at least I think I do. It's part of being taken care of, *discipline*. I've never had discipline, because I've never had anyone who cared enough. Not like *he* cares.

Discipline means caring.

The feeling in my heart makes more sense than the words sound in my head.

He beckons me closer. I step forward so slowly. "Take off your jeans," he says.

My heart thumps. "Okay, Daddy."

My fingers fumble because they're so shaky. I shimmy my jeans down my legs and step out of them, feeling so naughty as Daddy Nick stares at me in just my knickers. He's not smiling, not even a bit. His brows are so firm and serious.

He takes a seat in the armchair, his back upright and knees rigid. He pats his lap, and my legs are wobbly as I step over to join him. "Over my knee," he says.

I've never been over someone's knee before. I lower myself so tentatively, but he grabs me and hauls me into position, my ass raised so vulnerably on his lap. The shame makes me burn.

I squeak as he tugs my knickers down. They bunch around my knees, and it feels so naughty I screw my eyes shut.

"I'm doing this for your own good," he tells me, and his palm brushes my bare thigh. "Your own good, and mine, too." I manage

another nod. "This is going to hurt," he says, but I already know that.

The first slap takes me by surprise even though it shouldn't. I jolt forward on his lap, but he's got me. His arm presses onto my back to hold me steady while his other hand spanks me, and it hurts. It really hurts.

Daddy Nick hits hard.

"*Ow!*" I squeak. "*Ow, ow, ow...*"

My little shrieks don't do anything to put him off his stride. If anything it only makes him hit harder. It burns hot. Stings, too. Until the warmth begins to glow and tingle and my breathing slows from ragged gulps into long slow breaths.

"Naughty, careless, reckless little girl," he grunts, every word highlighted by a thwack of his palm.

I squeal when he slaps my thighs, and that makes the burn start up afresh. My hair swishes around my face with every blow, and his knees press into my hips as I teeter on his lap.

He tugs me closer for extra balance, and that's when I feel him. Feel how hard he is.

The burn on my ass spreads to my pussy. I want to clench my thighs but I don't dare.

He spreads my burning cheeks and I let out a gasp as his fingers slip round to my pussy.

"Is Daddy's punishment making you wet, Laine?" he asks. I'm not sure whether he wants me to be excited or not, so I don't say a word. He finds out for himself, slipping a finger inside me and moving it in and out. I'm sure he's left under no illusion. "Does making Daddy worried turn you on?"

"No!" I squeal. "No, Daddy! I just..."

"You just what?"

"I just..." I struggle to find the words. "I just like how it feels..."

He shifts underneath me. I guess that means he likes how it feels, too. His finger is still in my pussy, and I wish so hard he'd touch my clit and make me come.

"You're a naughty girl, Laine."

My face burns nearly as hot as my ass. "I'm sorry, Daddy," I whisper. "I didn't mean to be bad."

"I think you like your punishment, Laine. I hope this doesn't mean you'll misbehave for more."

"No." I shake my head. "I won't, I promise."

I like it more than I should, that's for sure. I guess I really am naughty.

"Say thank you to Daddy."

I don't know quite what he means until he eases me to the floor. His hand tangles in my hair and guides me to my knees before him, and he's loosening his belt and unbuttoning his trousers.

I stare at him with wide eyes, so embarrassed at how flushed and dishevelled I must look.

He pulls his cock free and he really is hard. The tip glistens, and I realise how much I must've been wriggling on his lap.

"I'm sorry, Daddy," I whisper as he guides it to my lips. "Thank you."

"What are you thankful for, Laine?"

I so want to answer correctly. "I'm thankful for… you teaching me… how to be a good girl."

"And teaching you to be a bad girl, too?"

"Yes, Daddy. And that."

"Suck me," he says and pushes his cock between my lips.

I've taken Daddy Nick in my mouth so many times by now, but not like this. His fingers hold my hair so tight, and he thrusts his hips so

hard that I retch around his cock. He doesn't let go, and I splutter and choke until my eyes stream.

"Good little girls suck Daddy's cock so sweetly," he grunts, but there's nothing sweet about the way I'm sucking him. Nothing sweet at all.

It's noisy and wet and slurpy, and spit dribbles down my chin and drips onto the floor. I'm unsteady with my knickers still bunched around my knees, and it gives him so much power to move me wherever he wants.

My head bobs like a doll's, my throat gurgling as he fucks my face, but I don't stop looking at him, don't stop wanting more.

"You really are a naughty little girl," he tells me, and I believe him. I really am a naughty girl. "Misbehave again and you'll get the belt," he threatens, and I know it's not an idle threat.

I wonder whether I'll like it as much as I liked his hand on my ass.

I wonder whether I'll ever get to find out.

"Daddy's going to come," he tells me. "Daddy's going to come in your naughty little mouth, Laine."

I squeeze my thighs together and it makes my clit spark.

I'm so ready for Daddy's come. I hope my eyes tell him so.

He thrusts to the back of my throat and swears under his breath, and I taste him. It makes me snort and that's full of cum, too. My eyes stream, but I don't care. I love being messy with Daddy Nick's cum.

I gulp in breath as he pulls out, and there's a stream of spit between the tip of his cock and my chin. He wipes it up with his thumb and sucks it into his mouth.

"Dirty girl," he says.

But I think Daddy Nick is the dirtiest one of all.

CHAPTER TWENTY THREE

Nick

I'm not sure how well Laine has learned her lesson, but she eats her dinner demurely and I have no reason to press the issue further.

I don't doubt she's sorry, and feel assured she won't be forgetting her phone again anytime soon. I know my possessiveness is irrational, and I'm fully aware that my punishment could be considered heavy-handed, but there's so much more at play within this situation.

I think my dirty little girl needed discipline as much as I needed to enforce it.

I decide to lighten the mood, gracing her with a smile as she forks up her carrots.

"I'd like you to accompany me to my work Christmas party," I tell her. "If you'd be happy to come along."

Her eyes light up, her fork paused halfway to her mouth. "Your party? Like a... date?"

"You'll be coming as my partner," I tell her. "I've already told my

colleagues about you."

"You have?" She looks so surprised.

"Of course I have, sweetheart. You're not a secret. I'm very proud to have you at my side."

A smile blooms on her face. "I'd like that."

"I'm glad," I tell her, and I am.

"Won't they think I'm too young? I mean, I look young…"

"They know how old you are."

She puts her fork back on the plate, carrots untouched. "Wow. I didn't expect…"

I reach for her wrist and squeeze. "Didn't expect what?"

She shrugs. "Just didn't expect… so much… I didn't know if you'd want your colleagues to know."

"I do," I tell her. "I'm very proud."

Her eyes sparkle. "Thanks, Daddy Nick. I'd really love to come to your party with you."

"Then we shall get you a dress." I smile. "A beautiful dress for my beautiful girl."

It's on the tip of my tongue to mention the necklace, but I leave it. Surprises are so special when they involve Laine.

"I've never been to a posh party," she admits. "I've never needed a proper dress."

"You're going to look stunning, Laine. I'll be the envy of every man there."

She looks so coy. So unaware of her own beauty.

"Thank you, Daddy," she says. "You're too good to me."

She's wrong, I'm not too good to her.

It's fate that's being too good to *me*.

***

Laine

I'm going to Daddy Nick's work party and I can't quite believe it. I'm so excited I could explode, and practically knock Kelly Anne off her feet as I grab her outside the college entrance.

"I'm going to a ball!" I tell her. "A real ball! With Nick! He's going to get me a pretty dress and I get to meet all his work colleagues. I'm really going to a ball!"

She looks just as unimpressed as I expected, but that doesn't matter. I just needed to say it out loud.

"I hope he's going to get you a pretty dress for my birthday party, too."

I could shrivel into nothing on the spot.

I should've asked Daddy Nick about Kelly Anne's party, but last night just didn't seem right. Not after I was in so much trouble for messing up already.

"I'll talk to him about it," I tell her and she groans.

"So you haven't told him?"

I shrug. "We were busy."

"*Busy*, right." She folds her arms. "Too busy to be bothered with the most important day of my year."

She's being a drama queen, and I can't be bothered to pander to it anymore. "I'll talk to him," I say, and leave it at that.

"Make sure you do," she says. "Besties before guys, that's the rule."

I fight the urge to laugh in her face.

She's never followed that rule in her life.

***

Nick

My framed print of Laine is waiting on my desk. It's perfect, just as I knew it would be. The frame is stylish and tasteful. A simple brushed silver lined with crackled pieces of blue shell that catch the light. It matches the blue of the butterfly magnificently.

I poke my head around the door to give Penny my thanks, and it startles her. "You're welcome, Mr Lynch," she says.

I'm about to retreat to my workload when she spins on her chair. She digs around in her desk drawer and hands me a set of keys.

"To the house you wanted fixing up," she explains. "It's all done. New locks, cleared of all the rubbish. I've had the walls freshly painted, and new floors laid where they couldn't be salvaged, which was pretty much everywhere." She pauses as she gathers her thoughts, mentally checking items off on her fingers. "I had to get new curtains for the living room and new blinds for the kitchen. Oh, and some new furniture. A new coffee table, sofa, and a couple of wardrobes. Oh, and some new cupboard doors for the kitchen units."

I turn the keys over in my hand. "Thank you, Penny. You've worked hard, I really appreciate it."

"That's my job," she says. It's very far from being her job and we both know it. She hands over an inventory of work done, and a pen for me to sign it off. "Shall I charge it to your expenses?"

I nod. "Please."

I sign without even checking the figures and it doesn't go unnoticed.

"It's Laine's house, right?" she questions.

"It *was* Laine's house."

Her smile is so friendly as she takes the documents back. "She's so much better off where she is now," she comments. "With you," she adds, as though there was any confusion.

"I'm glad you think so," I tell her, and I am.

I lock the keys in my desk drawer the minute I'm back in my office, and hope I never have cause to use them.

I never want Laine to go back there.

She belongs with me now.

***

I contemplate telling her about the house as we drive home, but I can't find the words. For all the rational control I have over my life, I'm aware that life still holds so many insecurities. The vulnerability of loving someone so much you're afraid of losing them. The vulnerability of Laine's old life being a viable alternative to the one we share.

She seems happy at my side, never any mention of the old house or how it's doing.

I suspect she's keen to stay in blissful ignorance, just as I am to keep her that way.

She glances in my direction. "Good day at the office?"

"Yes," I say. "Penny, my assistant, had the butterfly picture of you

framed for me. It's on my desk."

"It is? Really?"

"Really."

She giggles. "Now I can stare at you all day, even when I'm not with you."

"I like you staring at me, especially when I'm staring back."

"Me too," she says.

She's surprisingly quiet as I make dinner, pretending as usual to be absorbed in some assignment while her pen *tap tap taps* at her notepad. Something's clearly on her mind, and I wonder whether she's still fretting over her punishment last night.

"I need to ask you something," she tells me finally, and I stop stirring the pan to listen. "It's Kelly Anne's birthday on Saturday. She wants me to go. Out, I mean. Clubbing."

She's under no illusion as to what I think of Kelly Anne. Her pen taps all the faster.

"Clubbing?"

She nods. "Some drum and bass club on the beach front. I've told her I'm only interested in going for a couple of drinks."

"Kelly Anne leads you into trouble, Laine," I tell her.

"I know. But this time I won't let her."

"It sounds to me as though your mind is already made up."

"I won't go…" she says. "Not if you don't want me to. I'll tell her I can't."

"Do *you* want to go, Laine?" I keep my eyes on hers as I wait for her answer.

She shrugs, a usual response. "She's my friend. My only friend. I

always go out with her for her birthday."

"That's not what I asked."

She sighs. "I think I *should* go."

"Should and want are two very different things, sweetheart."

"She's my friend," she repeats. "She'll be so sad if I don't."

I very much doubt Kelly Anne has either the capacity or the loyalty to give a shit whether Laine is there or not after a couple of tequilas, but I keep that to myself.

"I'll need to know you're safe," I tell her, and she smiles.

"I'll stay safe, I promise."

"Midnight," I tell her. "I'll meet you at midnight, on the front by the pier. Insist she walks you back to the car, and make sure you keep your phone with you."

"I will." Her grin is so bright. "Thank you, Daddy Nick. I didn't think you'd let me go."

"It isn't a case of *letting* you do anything, sweetheart. You're free to make your own decisions, I'm just here to keep you safe."

"You do keep me safe," she says. "I never felt safe until I found you."

I only hope it stays that way.

I dish up our meal without another word.

***

Laine

Daddy Nick and I get ready for bed together every night. I'm brushing my teeth when he joins me to brush his, and I take a final pee

before sleep while he's finishing up.

He doesn't always wipe me, but he always watches. He's watching when I discover a healthy splotch of blood on the tissue paper.

My period.

My first period in this house.

He spits out his toothpaste and rinses his mouth. "We now know Daddy hasn't given you a situation along with his cum," he comments. "At least not yet, anyway."

I guess I should feel relieved, but I don't. I feel strangely sad.

"That's good, I suppose," I say, assuming that's the right response.

"Do you really think that's good?"

I wipe more blood away. "Yeah," I say, even though I don't think I mean it. "That's sensible, right?"

"I'm not worried about sensible, Laine, I'm interested in how you feel about it."

I don't really know how I feel about it, I tell him so. He kneels down beside me and wipes me afresh. It's become so normal, him doing this, I don't even flinch. "It needs some thought," he says. "If it's not something you're happy to risk, we'll have to use protection."

The idea of having him fuck me through a slimy condom doesn't sound horny at all. I like it, how we do it. I like feeling him, *only* him. I'm not interested in having a load of rubber inside me.

There's blood on my knickers, so Daddy Nick heads into my bedroom and finds me a fresh pair. He takes the pack of sanitary pads from my collection of toiletries and tears one open. I wonder if anyone else does this, but it's only a passing thought. I don't really care what anyone else does anymore, just as long as it's good enough for us.

I get to my feet and he slides my knickers up my thighs, complete with freshly placed pad. "That should keep you comfortable for the night," he says.

"I hope I don't ruin the sheets."

He smiles. "It doesn't matter if you do, sheets can be replaced, sweetheart."

That's not what I really want to say. I want to tell him there's an icky sadness in my belly, as though I was secretly rooting for something I didn't realise I wanted. I want to tell him that I've been having flutters doing my child development lectures at college and wondering how it would feel to have Daddy Nick's baby growing inside me.

I want to tell him that maybe it wouldn't be that bad. That maybe I'm more ready than I thought I was, want it far more than I ever expected it to.

I tell him nothing of the kind.

***

CHAPTER TWENTY FOUR

Laine

Kelly Anne pours us a sneaky vodka from her dad's bottle and tops it up with cheap cola. She clinks her glass against mine as she plays some drum and bass compilation I really don't like, as though simply having a bit of alcohol is cause for celebration. It doesn't feel like it. Not so much.

I've learned since her last birthday that some celebrations really mean something, but it seems Kelly Anne didn't get tagged in that particular life post.

"Gonna get so fucking trashed tonight!" she tells me, and my stomach rolls before I've even taken a sip. I have no doubt she's *gonna get so fucking trashed tonight*, only there's no way I'll be joining her in that. Not with Daddy Nick's Mercedes waiting like a pumpkin carriage as midnight strikes.

I've been telling her all week about my curfew. I didn't say it like that, that it's a curfew, just that we have plans. *Plans.* We do have plans actually. Nick is going to take me shopping for a Christmas party dress

tomorrow once the *birthday celebration* is done and dusted. He always says *birthday celebration* in that tone now when it comes to Kelly Anne. He says *everything* in that funny tone when it comes to Kelly Anne.

"Are you wearing *that*?" she asks, and I stare down at myself to work out exactly which *that* she's referring to. I'm dressed up, for me, wearing one of the sweet dresses Nick bought me and a pair of smart enough leggings underneath. He told me I looked beautiful, and I felt it. I'm not going to let Kelly Anne ruin that for me.

"I love this dress," I tell her.

"Sure, it's *nice*," she says. "But we're going *out*. Can't you wear something more dressy?"

Slutty, she means.

Her own black little number is up to her ass and barely covers her nipples.

I've actually been wondering how it would feel to wear something like that, but only for him, and only at home. Only when his eyes are dark and dirty and he wants me like *that*.

I definitely wouldn't want to wear it for a club full of drunk randoms, though.

"I love this dress," I repeat, and there's that confidence in my voice again that surprises me every time it comes out.

"Suit yourself," she says, and downs the rest of her drink.

I take another sip of mine and it tastes icky.

"You used to be more fun than this." She rolls her eyes. "This older guy crap is making you so dull, Laine."

Not so long ago it would have hurt to hear I was dull. Not so long ago I'd have tried my best to make her birthday the best night ever and downed that vodka with her and told her she looks amazing.

Being with Nick is changing me, she's right about that. I feel it right

the way through me, the way I have so much less time for her nasty opinions, or her whining about what I should and shouldn't be doing as her *bestie*. I didn't realise how many little conditions she has over every single thing we do together.

Nick has rules, but they're all for me, for *us*. Kelly Anne's silly rules are for nobody else but herself.

She checks herself in the mirror for the millionth time, and snaps a selfie and uploads it with a load of trendy hashtags for her fake friends on Facebook, and then she grabs her handbag.

"Come on, *bestieeeee*," she whoops. "It's party time!"

I can hardly contain my excitement.

***

Nick

I wish she hadn't gone. I wish she'd have decided for herself that her *friend* Kelly Anne treats her like a piece of shit on her shoe, keeping her close for the sake of vanity and little else.

It pains me that a selfish little cow like that has meant so much to my sweet Laine, but I'd dropped her at her friend's house and kissed her hair and told her to have a good time.

Some lessons in life need to be learned for yourself.

I keep an eye on the clock, even though it's barely scraped past eight. I keep my phone close by, just in case she calls and wants me to come for her, or if... anything else happens to her.

I concentrate on a month end report just to keep the paranoia at bay. The drunks, and the people popping pills, the people out for an easy fuck with little regard for who they take it from. All things that

my beautiful girl is too optimistic about human nature to avoid.

She always sees the best in everyone, and I love her for it. And it worries the shit out of me, knowing she's out there with the dregs of Saturday night partying with only a non-friend to watch her back, but still, I love her for her dedication in persisting with it.

Midnight.

I'll see her at midnight.

She has an alarm on her phone to let her know our rendezvous point is looming, and a fully charged battery – I checked before she left. She has enough money to get a taxi within a hundred mile radius, regardless of how many drinks Kelly Anne leeches out of her. And she has me.

I'll be waiting.

***

Laine

This club stinks. It's too loud to talk properly, not that I'd be talking anyway. Kelly Anne is already far more interested in some drunk guys than she is about me. Standard.

So much for *besties*.

So much for *Mason*, master of the female orgasm, too, seemingly.

I think about calling it off, making my excuses and heading back home to Nick where I belong.

Where I belong.

It's so nice to belong somewhere.

It's interesting that being out somewhere I hate makes it all the

more obvious how amazing my life is right now. I mean, I knew it. I know it every minute of every day, but *this*, this… fake pretence of having a good time… I'm really, really done with *this*.

This is the last crappy birthday party of Kelly Anne's I agree to. Next year she'll have to find some of her fake friends to hang out with. I'm done.

She introduces me to some wasted guy called Tyler, and I smile politely. Tyler tells me he's got pills, and I tell him thanks but definitely no thanks, and keep a close eye on my drink in case one of those pills magically ends up in there.

I keep an eye on Kelly Anne's drink, too, as hard as that is with her swinging it around all over the place as she flirts and grinds and makes a real slut of herself.

It's barely nine and I'm already bored to tears.

I'm thinking of my warm bed and Nick's kisses when Kelly Anne snatches my phone from my handbag.

"*Yeah… for real! Creepy old dude bought her this!*" She hands it to Tyler and his idiot friend, and I laugh into action that feels so alien to me. I try to grab it back, but Kelly Anne takes it from Tyler's hand before I can get to it. She holds it out of reach as she flicks through my phone gallery, and my privacy feels so personally invaded that I'm not sure whether I should slap her or cry or both. "*She's got a fucking curfew, too. Like Cinderella. Talk about creepy.*"

They laugh.

She laughs.

And for the first time in my life I really hate Kelly Anne.

I didn't even hate her when she left all my things with strangers and bailed on me, but right now, laughing about my life with Nick and treating me like a silly little joke, I hate her so much I want to storm out and never see her again.

If only I felt okay about leaving her with these creeps.

"Give it back!" I shout over the music. "It's not funny, Kelly Anne!"

She keeps flicking, as though she's got every right to snoop, and it irritates me so much I feel sick to my stomach. I have nothing private on there, not really, but that isn't the point. It really isn't the point.

She rolls her eyes when she sees I'm not playing, scrolling just a bit more to make a point before she hands it back.

My heart races as I check it for damage. There isn't any and I breathe in relief.

I check the time before I put it back to safety in my handbag, and it's only just gone eight o'clock. Shit.

The night is going to take forever.

***

Nick

I guess hearing nothing could be considered a good thing. Maybe she's really enjoying herself. Maybe Laine *likes* drum and bass. Maybe she likes dancing, too. I haven't yet had enough time to figure that out.

Maybe she's having so much fun with Kelly Anne that she's barely giving me a second thought, and as much as it pains me not to be the centre of her universe every waking minute, I'd be happy for her.

I want her to be happy. I want her to embrace life, and laugh and love and dance to drum and bass, if that's what makes her happy.

I keep working on my spreadsheet.

Just a few more hours to go.

***

Laine

Kelly Anne is too drunk to listen to anything much I have to say, but when I tell her at eleven that I might make a move early she seems to hear that loud and clear.

"NOOO!" she wails and grips my wrist for dear life. "I neeeeed you, bestie!"

Like hell she does.

She's grinding away on Tyler's friend Mickey, trying to smile so coyly like there's any chance she won't be fucking him this evening. Tyler is too close to me for comfort, dancing so close with a stupid grin on his face. I dance away a little, trying to keep a bit of distance, but wherever I go he follows.

"I'm serious!" I tell her. "I'm going soon, Kels! Nick will be waiting soon anyway!"

"I'm so sick of hearing about fucking Nick!" she snaps.

And I'm so sick of her bullshit and our one-sided friendship, but I bite my tongue and keep dancing.

It is her birthday, after all.

***

Nick

My heart is in my throat as the bell tolls midnight. I'm scouring the street, scanning the people walking from club to club for any sight of her beautiful blonde hair. I've parked up in the right spot, so there's no confusion where she should be headed, and I haven't had any news as to which exact club the girls have settled on, so I daren't leave my spot to head in her direction, just in case we cross paths and it leaves her in the cold.

It's snowing, just a little. The December air cold enough to numb my face. Just a few weeks from Christmas, and everyone is in high spirits, everyone except me.

I check my phone again. Nothing. I dial her number and it goes straight through to voicemail.

No big deal. A lot of the clubs don't have good phone reception, it could be nothing.

When my mobile shows it's ten past the hour I know I'm lying to myself.

***

Laine

"I'm really going now!" I tell her. I hold up my phone screen to show her the time. A quarter to midnight. Plenty of time to get back to the car.

I can't wait.

The night has taken forever.

Kelly Anne really is drunk now. She can barely stand up, gripping hold of my elbow as she presses her mouth to my ear. "There's no point," she tells me and her voice is slurry. The guys laugh, in on some secret joke at my expense, I'm sure.

"Whatever, Kels, let me take you home. I'm sure Nick won't mind."

She shakes her head and there's that cackle she gives me when she's being a bitch. "There's no point!" she laughs. "He won't *be* there!" She clinks her glass against mine. Mine's the same one I bought when we stepped in the place, and I have absolutely no intention of finishing it. I'm about to tell her that of course he'll fucking be there, but she's laughing so hard she wouldn't hear me. Someone walks over my grave, and I get this horrible sinking feeling, just like I did when I came out of the toilets and knew she was gone. "I changed your clock!" she laughs. "When I had your phone earlier! I changed the clock!"

My blood runs cold.

She squeezes my arm. "He makes you so *boring*, Laine! Curfew this and curfew fucking that. He's too fucking *old*! You should be having *fun!*"

I hate myself for being so stupid, holding up the handset to find it has no signal in this shitty place.

"You wouldn't..." I start, and I'm shaking my head, not really wanting to believe it, even though my gut knows it's true.

She holds up her own phone, and she's so proud. So fucking proud of her asshole move.

00:47

Shit. Nearly an hour late.

I wish the ground would swallow me up.

"Fuck you," I say, and I can't believe the words come out.

243

Her eyes are wide even through her drunkenness. "What?!"

"FUCK YOU!" I scream, and I don't care anymore. I push my way past her and head for the exit, pushing through the drunk idiots until I get to the cloakrooms, every step wobbly and desperate as my heart pounds and my handset tries fruitlessly to connect to the mobile network.

A hand on my arm nearly pulls me over, and for a second I'm back in the road as it rains, Daddy Nick's hand startling me from my panic.

Only it's not Nick. It's Kelly Anne, and she has the fucking gall to look pissed at me. "Don't fucking go!" she snaps.

"Leave me alone," I tell her. "Just leave me alone, Kels."

"It's *my* BIRTHDAY!" she screams. "You're my BEST FUCKING FRIEND!"

But I'm not.

She's no fucking friend of mine.

"I'm not your friend," I tell her. "You just use me to prop yourself up when there's nobody cooler."

She looks like I've slapped her, and I've got no time for this. I turn away from her but she won't let go. "No, Laine! *You* use *me* to prop yourself up! None of my other friends want to hang with me because of *you*." I don't want to hear it, but she won't let go of my wrist. "You know what they say about you, right? They call you *simple*. They call you *boring bitch*. Mary Vernon says you're so dull that you make her ears bleed. *That's* why I have no friends to hang out with, Laine! Because of *you*!"

It hurts.

It hurts like she intends it to.

But not nearly so much as knowing I missed my curfew.

"Fuck you, Kelly Anne, I'm done," I tell her. I'm calm and I mean it. I really fucking mean it.

244

I tug away from her and head for the street, and this time she doesn't follow me.

"HE DOESN'T FUCKING LOVE YOU!" she screams. "NOBODY DOES!"

***

CHAPTER TWENTY FIVE

Laine

I've never run so fast in my life. My feet barely touch the floor as I pound the beach front, my heart in my throat as I realise what I've done. What *she's* done.

I'm out of breath as I see his car in the distance, but I still keep running, and then I see him, and he's running too.

I slam into his body and wrap my arms around his neck and I want to tell him how sorry I am but no words will come.

"What, Laine?! What is it? What's going on?" His hands are in my hair, on my cheeks, checking me all over, and his eyes are wide and petrified.

I struggle for breath, and it pains so much to see what I've done.

"Nothing…" I wheeze. "Not like that… it was Kelly Anne! She changed my clock! I didn't know! I swear I didn't know!"

His eyes are so hurt as he realises. So hurt.

It makes me feel like shit upon shit. I struggle not to cry, but I don't deserve to cry, not after being so stupid. I've been so stupid.

I really am naive. Just a stupid fucking idiot. Just like Kelly Anne says.

"You gave her your phone?" he asks, and it's so angry and pointed that my tummy flips.

"No! She took it! I wouldn't! I didn't!"

"I've been waiting here an hour, Laine. A whole fucking hour." He's so hurt, his eyes so scared. "I was out of my fucking mind, Laine! Petrified! Do you have any fucking idea what that's like? Do you have any fucking idea?"

No. I don't.

Because I've never lost anybody. Not like he has.

But I'm beginning to get a sense of it. Because I'm petrified of losing him right now. Petrified of losing everything.

"I'm sorry," I whisper, and my voice sounds pathetic and small. "I'm so sorry, Nick."

There's no *Daddy* this time, but he doesn't even notice. He's staring past me, into the distance, his jaw gritted and his eyes so sad.

"Get in the fucking car," he says.

***

Nick

A terrible concoction of relief and anger. Hurt, too.

Hurt that someone as loving and special as Laine could do something so stupid and reckless.

My temples pound as I drive, my gut churning and twisted.

"I'm sorry," she says again, but it does nothing to calm my mood.

I have nothing to say, not like this. Not while I'm still wired and on the edge, chased by demons I've tried so hard to ignore. Demons that know exactly how it feels to lose everything.

I pull through the gates and park up, slam the car door as I head for the front door. Laine follows like a shadow, her fingers clasped tight together and her eyes on the floor.

I close the door behind us, and then I lock it, barricading us in as though she's still in danger.

Only she wasn't in danger, only reckless. Trusting. Far too trusting.

"I'm sorry," she whispers. "I'm so sorry, Nick, I swear."

I pour her a juice, unsure of how much she's had to drink already, and dig out a bottle of whisky from my father's vintage stash and pour myself a healthy measure. She watches me, staring with big doe eyes.

"I can go," she whispers. "If you want… I can go…"

"You aren't going fucking anywhere!" I snarl. "Not fucking anywhere, Laine. You're fucking grounded! Forever, Laine, for-fucking-ever!"

Grounded. It sounds so fucking stupid.

She nods anyway. "Okay."

"No!" I snap. "It's not okay, Laine! It's really not okay!"

I stare at the girl in front of me, only she's not a girl, not really. I can't keep her in a cage, can't protect her from everything, can't keep pretending she's an infant who needs me to dress her and wash her and wipe her dirty ass.

It all falls away, this illusory game we're playing.

She's not Jane.

She's not Louisa, either.

She's just her. A young woman who's never known love. Who's never known what it feels like to be cared for.

And that's what she wants from me.

She wants love. Not just kinky daddy play, or a new phone, or a daily call at lunchtime. She wants love. Actual love, as an actual young woman with someone who treats her right.

"Talk to me," she whispers. "Please."

I don't know where to start.

She takes a step closer and her eyes are so eager for reassurance. "Please talk to me."

"I was scared," I tell her. "So scared I couldn't think straight."

She nods. "I was scared too. Scared because I knew how scared you'd be. Scared because I'd hurt you so bad." Her lip trembles. "Scared because I thought I'd lost everything, all for the sake of someone who never even gave a shit about me. Scared I'd ruined the only good thing I've ever had."

Her words pang. "You haven't lost anything, Laine. I'm still right here. I'm just fucking angry."

She nods. "Angry because of me. Scared because of me."

"Scared because of that stupid selfish bitch Kelly Anne more specifically."

She shrugs. "I should have stopped her. Should have checked."

"Yes," I agree. "You should have."

"It'll never happen again..." she says.

"No," I tell her. "It won't."

She sips at her juice, and she's thinking, her gaze darting around the room as she tussles with some course of action or another. "You could punish me," she says. "Like your father did, with the belt. I deserve it, Daddy. I deserve everything."

I feel the beast stir, taking advantage of the adrenaline. It's so easy to want that. So easy to seek out control in the way I learned from my father and he learned from his. The belt is hanging on the hook behind the study door, in the same place he used to keep it.

The prospect of tanning Laine's pretty little backside and making her suffer for her recklessness is so fucking tempting.

"Never angry," I tell her. "My father never disciplined me in anger, Laine."

"But your father never lost anyone," she whispers. "Not like you did."

That's true enough.

"I don't mind," she says. "Really, Daddy, I don't mind."

Her eyes are so adoring, so eager to make it all better. Maybe the belt would do that, forge a bond of respect that no silly little bitch like Kelly Anne will ever stand a chance of breaking.

"It'll hurt," I tell her, and she nods.

"I know it will, Daddy."

"You don't," I say. "You don't know at all."

"I don't care," she says.

I down the rest of my whisky.

"Go through to the study," I tell her.

***

Laine

My nerves are on fire, tummy churning so bad I feel like I could

throw up, but I make my way along the hallway and open the door to the study without a single moment's hesitation.

I want this. I want to please Nick and make him feel better. I want to make him feel safe. I want him to know I really am a good girl.

I want him to know that I really am sorry.

He isn't far behind, and my breath catches as he closes the door behind us. The belt swishes on the hook as it slams, and I wonder if I'm really ready for this.

"Over the desk," he tells me. "On your front."

I lower myself so carefully, pressing my cheek to the leather inlay. It smells rich and woody, like old books and scotch.

I imagine Nick here, in this very same position. I wonder if his heart used to race like mine is now.

He lifts my dress, and tugs down my leggings and my knickers without saying a word.

The air feels cold. My skin feels prickly.

My mouth feels so dry I can hardly swallow.

"Six," he says. "I'm going to give you six. Not because I'm angry, but because you deserve it."

"Naughty girls need discipline," I whisper.

"Discipline shows care, Laine."

"I know," I tell him. "I know, Daddy Nick."

"I love you, Laine," he tells me and I'm so sad for what I've done that it hurts more than his belt ever could.

"I love you too, Daddy."

"Six," he repeats. "And you'll learn your lesson."

I've already learned it, but that doesn't matter. Nothing matters but *us*. Nothing matters but loving Nick and him loving me back. Nothing

matters but making sure I never hurt him again.

I gasp as the leather glides across my ass cheeks. "This is going to hurt," he says. He gives me a tap, and the leather feels so smooth against my bare skin.

I wonder how many times it's been used for this.

I hold my breath. Grip the edge of the desk so tightly.

And then I wait.

Silence.

One long empty silence.

"I love you so much, sweetheart," he whispers.

And then he hits me.

I squeal and jolt forward on the desk, and my breath catches.

It scars. It really fucking sears.

Burns so bad I fidget from foot to foot.

"One," he says.

I don't want two, and I know it.

I really don't want two.

I cry out when it lands, and it sounds so pathetic and desperate.

The tears come so easily, filling my eyes and spilling over.

"Two," he says, and my body jolts with these crazy sobs that make me feel like a baby. "You understand why I'm doing this?" he asks.

I nod. I do understand.

I asked for it. In every sense of the word.

I squeal again when it lands for the third time.

A baby, I'm such a fucking baby.

"Three."

I lurch forward and wail like a banshee as four strikes, and my ass is on fire.

"Four."

I cry openly at the next, no longer caring how I look, or if I take my punishment well for him.

I don't care about anything much apart from the burn.

"Five."

I close my eyes for six. And he waits.

He waits until my sobs ease, and my body stops shaking.

He waits until I twist my head to look at him and blink through the tears.

"Have you learned your lesson, Laine?" he asks and I nod.

"Yes, Daddy."

He drops the belt.

No six.

It makes the tears come all the harder.

And this time he's there. Pulling me up and holding me and smoothing my hair as I cry.

I have no right to cry, but Daddy Nick doesn't seem to care about that. Daddy Nick is so warm and kind.

So loving, even when I've caused him so much pain.

"I told you it would hurt," he says, and I nod against his chest, my wet eyes soaking through the fabric of his shirt.

I hope I don't snot on him, but I doubt he'd care so much anyway.

He puts his hands on my cheeks and tips my face to his and his eyes aren't angry anymore, just scared.

"I'll never use the belt on you again," he says. "You're not a little girl, Laine. We just like to pretend you are."

A strange sob from my throat, and I'm nodding. I'm really nodding.

And I'm happy, and sad, and relieved, and scared, and everything in between.

"Thank you, Nick," I say.

***

CHAPTER TWENTY SIX

Nick

Laine needed to be cared for, just as I needed to care for her. Both needing that special someone to slot so nicely into their broken parts.

It was beautiful.

It still is beautiful.

But this game can't be all we are, not anymore.

I pour her a whisky as I pour myself one. "It'll help calm you down," I say.

She manages a smile.

I take a seat at the table opposite and we sit in a silence no longer simmering with conflict.

We're past that now.

My demons have backed away into their shadowy pit, and the girl in front of me no longer looks like her soul is breaking.

"Tell me about Kelly Anne," I say. "Not just about what a cow she is, but about why you ever liked her in the first place."

"You really want to know?"

I nod. "I really want to know. It was part of you, Laine. I want to understand why. Maybe that way we can stop it ever happening again."

"It won't happen again anyway. I'm done with her."

I believe her. Her eyes are full of the pain of betrayal.

I know it's a tough pill to swallow.

She takes a moment, spinning the empty tumbler on the table as she clears her head.

I understand that well enough, because I'm still clearing mine too.

"I didn't have anyone," she says. "I was shy when I started school. I'd never done nursery, or been around other kids before. It was always just me and Mum, and I was scared all the time, worried that she wasn't coming back." She smiles sadly. "Mainly because she didn't come back sometimes. Men, or work, or whatever. She'd leave me with the neighbour. An old woman who smelled of cheese."

"Cheese?"

"Green cheese." She wrinkles her nose. "She was nice enough but she really stunk."

"And Kelly Anne was there?"

She nods. "Kelly Anne was a bossy boots. I felt so safe with her, because she wasn't scared of anything."

"And she was nice to you?"

She shrugs. "Most of the time. I'd follow her around even when she was bored of me. She'd play with other kids, and I'd just watch. Waiting until they argued, because she'd argue with people a lot, and make sure I was there to pick up the pieces. I made sure I was useful, just so she'd keep me around."

"That's not friendship, Laine. Not really."

"I know that now," she says. "But I never wanted to see it that way before. I never wanted to look at it. It's impossible to carry on doing what you've always done if you realise it's full of bullshit and lies."

"I get that," I say. "You wanted it to be real."

"Yeah," she says. "I guess I did." She spins the glass. "Kelly Anne was always so selfish. She was only really interested in what she wanted. Where she wanted to go or what she wanted to play or who she wanted to fuck. I was just an accessory, like a handbag. She'd tell me stories and make them sound so amazing. I guess she felt so cool knowing I was so not."

"Cool means shit, sweetheart."

"I think I know that now, too." She smiles a sad smile at me. "The more cooler she seemed, the older she seemed. The more childish I felt, the safer I felt. Same with Mum. Only Mum really couldn't take care of herself, not around work and all her men trouble. So I had to be a mum to Mum. A mum to her and a silly little sad friend to Kelly Anne, and somewhere it all got messed up."

"Life can get all messed up, Laine. But we can straighten it out again."

A tear rolls down her cheek. "I hope so. Because I'm happier than I've ever been. I didn't know what it would feel like to have someone who really loved me. I didn't know how safe I'd feel with someone who could take care of me."

"I feel safe too," I admit. "I feel safe when I believe I have control over a situation. Over you. But I don't. I don't have control over you, Laine, and that's alright. I shouldn't ever have control over who you are, or what you want to do. I can support you, I can care for you, but not control you."

She doesn't look convinced, but I am.

Love has to be free. Alive like a butterfly, not pinned to a mount

like the specimens I've been keeping for so long.

Jane's room was the perfect bell jar. Preserved so perfectly, just waiting for me to fill it with another little girl to replace the one I lost.

A second chance at the same dream.

Only no two dreams can ever be the same.

"I love you," she says. "I really love you. Not because of what you do for me, but because you're honest and caring and see everything I want to see in myself."

"I love you too, Laine. Not because you're my little girl, or because we share some weird kink that nobody else understands. I love you because you have a beautiful soul."

She smiles so brightly. "I don't need Kelly Anne anymore."

I reach for her hand across the table and squeeze. "Jane's gone," I tell her. "Louisa, too. And I'm ready to let them rest now, Laine. We're different."

"We're *us*," she says. "I want to be *us*."

"So do I, sweetheart."

Her fingers look so small in mine. "So, what now?"

"We go to bed," I tell her. "Tomorrow is a new day."

She nods. "I'd like that very much."

***

Laine

I feel like I've cried for a lifetime as I wash my face in the bathroom. My cheeks are puffy and my eyes are tired.

But I feel good. Like I've dumped a horrible weight.

I guess Kelly Anne's been nothing but a drain on me for longer than I can remember.

I wonder how different life would have been if I'd have stopped clinging onto her all those years ago. I wonder if I'd have made other friends, lived another life.

I wonder if I'd have grown up.

I feel like I'm growing up now.

And that's weird. It seems so silly that being cared for as a child was what turned me into a woman.

I smile to myself and Nick smiles back.

"What a day," he says.

"I'm pooped," I tell him, and he nods.

"Me too."

I hold his hand as he steps onto the landing, waiting for him to open Jane's door like he always does. But not today.

He steps on past, and my heart pounds as he opens a different door. The one to his room.

I've barely ever been in there.

He flicks on the bedside light and pulls back the covers for me.

"This is my bed," he tells me, like it needs explaining. "I'll clear out some wardrobe space for you in the morning."

I nod. "Thanks."

It feels so weird to slip into his grown up sheets. They're grey. So stylish and grown up.

And soft.

They're soft, too.

He pulls me close and kisses my hair, and I know he'll never be

Daddy Nick in this place. It just doesn't fit.

And that feels okay.

It feels just fine.

"Goodnight, Laine," he says and the words roll off my tongue so easily.

"Goodnight, Nick."

He squeezes me a little bit tighter, and I know we're going to be just fine.

***

CHAPTER TWENTY SEVEN

Laine

It's strange to wake in such a big bed, but there's so much more room for stretching out in. I kick out my legs and enjoy the space, and Nick is right beside me with a quiet smile on his face.

"Morning, sleepyhead."

"Morning, Nick."

Nick.

It's going to take some getting used to. How funny, how things change. We've been on a rollercoaster, him and I. It climbed so high so fast, and then it tumbled, so scary as the train sped over the drop. But we're still on the rails, and somehow I think we'll be climbing even higher this time.

It's late, I can tell by the light at the window. I take in the surroundings, and it's nice in here, in his space. I like it.

I look at the bedside cabinet on my side and wonder what I'll fill it with. I wonder which wardrobe I'll hang my clothes in, and if it would

be appropriate to bring Mr Ted in here too.

"Are you hungry?" he asks.

I shake my head, and I'm not today. I'm really not.

I stroke his face, my thumb brushing over his shadowy stubble, and I want him so much it makes my toes curl.

"I know that expression," he tells me, and kisses my fingers.

And I know his.

I'm coming to know everything. Every one of his smiles.

And his frowns. I've seen a few of those now too.

He kisses me and his lips are soft and warm. His tongue is gentle today, tasting me so slowly. I breathe into him and tangle my fingers in his hair, my legs reaching for his, my knee hooking under and guiding him close.

It feels so natural, the way he moves, positioning himself above me with his weight on his elbows. I hook my ankles around his calves, and my body knows how this works now. It knows how to tip my hips just right and how to shift myself underneath him.

He's so hard, rubbing himself just right, the length of him pressed just where I need him.

But I don't want it like this today. I want it to be different. *New.*

I smile as I push my hand to his chest, loving the way his eyes show such surprise as I wriggle out from under him and urge him to move.

Nick looks so different on his back, his cock so proud as I work it in my fingers.

I suck him, and he groans. He raises his arms and rests them behind his head, and his legs part so willingly.

He's mine.

And today this is my show, my way.

It feels amazing to be in control.

Kelly Anne was wrong about sex, just like she was wrong about so many things I took her word on.

To be sexy doesn't mean you have to wear a short skirt and bright red lipstick. It doesn't mean you have to do a striptease or put on some epic performance.

It just means being confident. Being yourself.

Being sexy means being *me*.

And today I want to be me. I'm good enough for Nick to love me, and that makes me good enough for me too.

I've never been on top before. It feels so alien to straddle him, but I like it.

I play with my clit and he watches without moving. His eyes are dark, but not fierce, even though he lets out the same low groan as I position his cock and lower myself onto him.

I move just as I want to, my hips circling and my little tits bouncing just as much as they can bounce, and the pressure inside builds so easily this way.

It feels amazing.

Everything feels amazing.

"Beautiful," he says, and I feel it. I do feel beautiful, so exposed and on display.

I lean forward, and kiss him, and the angle is just right. It must be right for him too, because his breath is fast and ragged, and his hips thrust right back at me.

"Fuck," he groans. "Fuck, Laine, that feels incredible."

I know it does. It feels perfect. Perfect enough that my movements are frantic and my thighs are tense.

I'm going to come, and I know that, but it's different. This feels

different.

Bigger and deeper and…

And fuck.

Fuck.

Oh, fuck. Fuck, fuck, fuck.

I don't know if I've said it aloud and I don't care. My senses are fried, my nerves sparking like crazy, and my whole fucking body shudders.

And then he comes too.

And I feel it. I feel it so well in this position.

I did it.

I did it all and I'm so proud.

He pulls me into his arms and holds me tight, and I giggle. I can't stop giggling.

He holds me until I'm quiet, and then he brushes the hair from my forehead, stares at me with eyes that let me know he enjoyed it as much as I did.

"You must be hungry now," he says.

***

Nick

I absolutely refuse to express an opinion until Laine has whittled her dress choice down to three. I want it to be her decision, exactly the dress she wants.

She's surprised me, but that in itself isn't surprising. She's always

surprising me.

Her three choices are so grown up. Tasteful gowns in dark colours, rich navy or mulled wine.

I can hardly contain myself as she slips into the dressing room to try them on, and when she steps out in the blue dress I lose the power of speech.

She really does take my breath away.

"I like it," she tells me. "I like it a lot." She smiles. "In fact, I think I love it."

She does a twirl and the fabric swishes. It's highlighted with diamante, tiny little stones that look like stars on a night sky.

"I think I love it, too," I tell her. "Very much." I sigh. "You look gorgeous, Laine."

"This is the dress," she says. "I just know it."

She turns around for my help with the zip, and it's so nice to brush my fingers down her spine.

"Then we'd better go pay for it," I say.

***

I've never been so proud as I am to have my beautiful Laine on my arm at the Christmas party.

Her eyes are still bright and shining with innocent wonder, but my little girl isn't a little girl, not with her makeup on.

She's most certainly a young woman this evening.

Michael French hands her a glass of champagne, and nudges me to convey his approval.

"I've heard so much," he tells her. "All good, of course."

"I'm so pleased to meet you," she says, and she means it, I can tell.

"This is my wife, Barbara, and my daughter Caroline." I smile as warmly as she does, and it thrills me as Caroline strikes up conversation.

Maybe they really could be friends.

I'd like my sweet Laine to have nice friends.

"They're so nice!" she gushes and lands a kiss on my cheek. "Caroline said she's here for weeks until she's back at uni, suggested we go to theirs for their Boxing Day party."

"Would you like that?"

She nods. "I'd love that. I love meeting your friends, Nick."

I'm certain they love meeting her, too. Penny and Mike, and Trevor from IT. So many people I've seen every day and given no thought to whatsoever.

That's all going to change.

I'm going to change. Hell, we've changed so much already, Laine and I.

I think there'll be plenty of new developments this coming year, not least the little bump Laine seems eager to have in her belly.

We've talked about it properly, just like we should have done before I unloaded my cum into her pussy at every opportunity.

She's young, but not that young, and I'm certainly not getting any younger myself.

I still want to be able to do everything good fathers do.

I want to trek through the countryside with our butterfly nets, and be there for them until they're plenty old enough to take care of themselves.

I have time, but it's ticking.

The necklace is a sly little test. I present it in its sweet little box, and watch her expression as I open it.

The disappointment is only fleeting, but it's there.

A necklace not a ring.

But it's beautiful, and the thinks so too.

"Oh, Nick… Oh my God…"

"A diamond for my sweetheart," I tell her, and step behind her to fasten it around her neck. "I can't take the credit," I admit. "Penny chose it. You'll have to thank her for her excellent taste."

"I'm thanking *you*," she says. "I'll show you how much I love it later."

And then she heads off to find Penny.

Her new-found confidence amazes me.

Everything about her amazes me.

Somehow I think Barbara French really will need to be buying a hat for our big day.

And soon.

Very soon.

I can't wait until my sweet little Laine Seabourne is sweet little Laine Lynch.

***

EPILOGUE

Laine

He tells me my old house is finished. Good as new he says.

I kick off my heels and thank him, but it feels so far away that place.

I guess it will be nice for Mum should she ever come back.

Maybe she'll be back for Christmas. Maybe I'll get a text.

Maybe she'll even come to dinner with Nick and me.

Maybe I don't really care that much anymore.

I'm excited about my own life now.

I'm excited about finishing up my college course, even though Nick tells me he earns enough for both of us. For *all* of us. For the children we plan to have and the life we want to lead. Enough for *everything*.

At least child studies puts me in an alright position to have babies

of my own.

I want so many of Nick's babies.

He says he's going to redecorate Jane's room. A new room for new little people when they come along.

He's already started boxing up her things.

He's moved her DaDDy drawing to the corkboard in the pantry. I trace my fingers around the letters sometimes, and wonder what it will be like to have a little girl of my own someday.

Nick threw the belt from the study into the fire, said he doesn't need that anymore either.

He says that discipline doesn't need to be cruel to be kind, and some rules are made to be broken. That's life he says.

The thought of his hand on my ass still gives me tickles, and I think that maybe I'll have to be a naughty girl some time, just to go over his knee again.

I really am dirty these days, and that's ok too.

I've been trying to find a way to tell him. Trying to find a way to show him what I want without it feeling icky.

I mean how icky can it be to play a little when you've got someone's engagement ring on your finger? It doesn't get much more grown up than that.

I've only got a bit of time left before Jane's pink room is all gone. Her bed is still there and her pink curtains too, but they won't stay. Not forever.

My pink robe still hangs on the back of the door, even if her fairy castle has been put away in the garage. I have a new robe now, and it's purple, not pink.

I even have lacy underwear these days too. If I could forgive Kelly Anne enough to speak with her, I'm sure she'd laugh.

I help Nick chop up the vegetables for dinner, and my engagement ring sparkles in the light. I stop to stare and he grabs me from behind, lands hot kisses on the back of my neck until I squeal.

"Less of the magpie act, more chopping please, sweetheart," he says. "I'm looking forward to an early night."

I am, too.

I've been craving an early night all week.

It's the right time, my ovulation app tells me so.

I hope tonight's the night his cum gives me a little baby of our own.

He leads me upstairs when we're done eating, and I still follow so close to him, ever his little shadow.

His fingers squeeze mine as he heads for our bedroom, but I stop, my heels digging into the carpet.

He turns back and stares at me, his eyes dark in the way I love so much.

"What is it?" he says.

I smile so shyly, and my cheeks burn. My clit so tickly as I think about my guilty little pleasure.

I've been thinking about it a lot lately.

"I just… I was thinking…"

"Spit it out, sweetheart," he says. "No secrets, remember?"

I nod, then glance at Jane's door, and he knows. He just knows.

He's smiling as he steps closer, and I'm smiling too as he hitches up the hem of my dress.

"I see," he says, and he does see.

His eyes burn as he stares at my plain cotton knickers, white, just as he liked so much.

"Have you been a naughty girl, Laine? Thinking dirty thoughts about Jane's sweet pink bed?"

My breath hitches. My clit tickles.

"Maybe..." I say.

"Maybe?"

I smile. "Maybe a little..."

I worry that maybe he's done with this, maybe it will be too weird for him with us trying for a baby and all, and I suddenly feel an idiot for pulling a stunt like this without asking, and maybe I should've-

His lips stop my mind whirring, and his tongue is so fierce just like it used to be.

He squeezes my nipples, pinching them just enough to make me gasp, and he's groaning, hard against my belly his thigh presses between mine and rubs.

"We don't have to..." I begin, just to be sure. "I mean, if it's weird, Nick, we don't have to... I just thought... for fun..."

His eyes are darker than I've seen them in weeks. His smirk dirty enough to make my tummy tickle.

"Call me Daddy," he says, and opens the door.

***

THE END

Jade West

276

ACKNOWLEDGEMENTS

As always, so many people to thank.

My incredible editor, John Hudspith, who really pulled out all the stops on this, as always. Johnny, for real, this was an amazing ride. I couldn't do this without you.

Letitia Hasser, for the insanely awesome cover. RBA Designs, everyone. Such talent!

Tracy Smith Comerford, for being my constant sounding board and working like a trooper.

Michelle McGinty and Lesley Edwards, for your support as always.

Louise Ramsay, your beta feedback is always so insightful.

My dirty girls and boys, I love you all, and the group makes me smile so hard.

To all the amazing authors I'm lucky enough to call my friends, and all the bloggers and readers who so tirelessly support me. You are

all amazing. I'm both grateful and honoured.

My friends, who put up will all my incessant book talk and crazy sleep schedule. Maria, Lisa, Dom, Hanni, Kate, Marie, Tom, Jo, James, Siobhan… some of you so near and some of you so far… I love you all.

My family. Mum, Dad, Brad, Nan, Julie, Jenny, and of course, Jon. You are everything.

To anyone I've missed, I'm sorry. I've had about four hours sleep this week and my brain is fried.

A huge, huge thanks to my author buddies, Isabella Starling and Demi Donovan, who deserve a mention all of their own.

These ladies, wow. I've been lucky enough to have them here for a week of writing, and they have absolutely rocked my world.

I've laughed so much my nose literally bled, and I haven't had a nosebleed since I was a kid.

Yeah, it was intense. And fun. So much fun.

We've talked, we've written, we've barely slept, and I'm honoured to have had such incredible company while sprinting to the finish line of this novel.

It was quite a sprint.

And this was quite a week.

I can't wait to do it again. <3

ABOUT JADE WEST

Jade has increasingly little to say about herself as time goes on, other than the fact she is an author, but she's plenty happy about it. Spending her time in imaginary realities and having a legitimate excuse for it is really all she's ever wanted.

Jade is as dirty as you'd expect from her novels, and talking smut makes her smile.

She lives in the Welsh countryside with a couple of hounds and a guy who's able to cope with her inherent weirdness.

She has a curio cabinet, a living room decorated with far more zebra print than most people could bear, and fights a constant battle with her addiction to Coca-Cola.

Find Jade (or stalk her – she loves it) at:

http://www.facebook.com/jadewestauthor

http://www.twitter.com/jadewestauthor

http://www.jadewestauthor.com

Made in the USA
Coppell, TX
26 May 2021

56270314R00164